SOLD TO THE HIGHEST BIDDER

BY: MISTY A NESLEN

ISBN: 979-8-89324-886-9

Published by Franklin Publishers

Printed in the United States of America

For permissions, inquiries, or additional copies, contact:

Franklin Publishers

www.franklinpublishers.com

CONTENT GUIDANCE

This novel explores aspects of Human trafficking, murder, violence, including Physical and emotional abuse, confinement, and forced relationships. Please read with care.

DEDICATION

To all the quiet girls with stories in their heads.

To those who bend but don't break,

and who always seem to find themselves in the books they read

TABLE OF CONTENTS

01

MEETING HIM...

After passing through the glass door, I cheerfully announce myself to no one in particular. "Good Morning!" I noticed Jenny standing near her locker and smiling.

"Good morning, Sophia. Can you believe the VIP ball starts tonight? I am so pumped for it..." Jenny says as she tugs her small tie around her neck. I settled on the bench, watching her lightly straighten her uniform and pop her lips as she carefully drew lipstick across them. Jenny and I have been through so much together—aging out of the system, facing the challenges of adulthood, and learning how to navigate life on our own. Our bond runs deep, built on shared struggles and the unwavering support we've given each other. Seeing her like this, preparing herself with such care, reminds me of how far we've come and how much we've leaned on each other to get here.

We both found a job at the King's Court, which is an upscale, luxurious hotel located in sunny Los Angeles, California. This hotel is owned by Morelli Incorporated, which also owns other hotels, banks, trading companies, and other affiliate companies located overseas. The VIP ball, an annual event of great prestige hosted by

Morelli Incorporated, has always been a highlight overseas. This year, however, Morelli Incorporated chose our hotel as its venue, a decision that filled us with both honor and responsibility. The entire staff has poured their hearts into ensuring every detail is perfect for tonight's celebration. The grand ballroom buzzes with energy as opulent chandeliers are meticulously adorned with shimmering glass shards, creating a display of breathtaking beauty. Exquisite floral arrangements are carefully placed, transforming the space into a haven of elegance. Meanwhile, the cooks have crafted a sumptuous feast, their dedication and skill evident in every dish. Tonight, the hotel shines not just with lights and flowers, but with the pride and effort of everyone involved.

"Oh, I know it is exciting. I'm sure you will have a busy night since you work in the casino. I'm pretty sure most of the guests will find their way there." I replied to her with a smile. Although Jenny got the job I wanted, the guy who interviewed me felt I wasn't cut out for the role. In his opinion, my innocent demeanor and face would be a better fit for working at the reception desk. At first, I was disappointed, but I have come to appreciate the receptionist role more than I expected at first. It allows me to interact with a wide variety of guests, and I've discovered I have a knack for making them feel welcome.

"True, but you get to see them all first," she replied as she applied lipstick in one of the many mirrors in the room. "I, on the other hand, will meet them after they've had some alcohol, and all the men only ever seem to want one thing. Especially the rich assholes that come here."

I nodded at her, understanding what she said. "I'm sorry, Jenny. I wish I could help. But remember, I understand, because I work at the reception desk. Who do you think they call for every little whim they want?" I replied. "We both have demanding roles in this place. We'll get through it. Just as we have for the past three weeks."

"I know, and I appreciate that you do," she said, turning to face me with a small smile. "It's just exhausting sometimes, you know? But you're right, we'll get through it together. We always do." I sit on the bench and slip on my shoes. "Wait, what if one of those assholes sees me and falls in love with me at first sight?" she suddenly squeals out.

I laugh, "You know love doesn't work like that. Besides, would you really want to be stuck with an asshole like that?" I ask smiling.

Jenny pauses for a moment, considering my words. "Oh, I guess you're right," she admits, her expression softening. "But sometimes it is fun to imagine a fairytale moment, even if reality is far from it." She shrugs, a playful glint in her eyes, and we both share a lighthearted moment before heading to our respective posts. Heading into the lobby, I immediately noticed a large crowd gathered near the front door. I could see several well-known reporters in the crowd. Then I saw famous people exiting their limos before entering the hotel doors. "Oh my god,... Sophia, look... Look who just got out of that limo?" Jenny screamed, grabbing my shoulder and shaking me in her excitement. "They call him the King around here; he's always on the VIP list, no matter where he travels." The lobby buzzed with anticipation, the air thick with excitement and curiosity as the crowd craned their necks to catch a glimpse of the celebrities. Flash bulbs popped like fireworks, casting brief, dazzling light flares across the room. The hum of whispering conversation and the occasional gasp of recognition filled the space, creating a vibrant, electric atmosphere that pulsed with life.

"What? Where? My eyes scanned the famous people walking into the building as I asked, "Who?". Even though I hate celebrity gossip, I couldn't resist joining her in seeing the man. He was tall with a confident stride, his hair perfectly styled, and wearing a tailored suit that seemed to shimmer in the light. His presence commanded attention, and it was clear why everyone was captivated by him. He was surrounded by beautiful, prestigious women. On his left were two very famous supermodels, both dressed elegantly and well-known. On his right was a beautiful and extremely popular actress in a glamorous dress. All of the women around him were gorgeous.

"I heard he lives in the penthouse suite, and that he's been there for a while now," Jenny says, watching as he walks by, admiring how he glides along. I widened my eyes at her.

"Wait a minute, a single night in that room costs several thousand dollars!" I admitted. I suddenly wondered what this man did to afford the penthouse suite. I couldn't take my eyes off him as he walked by.

"OMG... look, Drago is here!" I suddenly hear a girl screech from behind me, before everyone around me shrieks and the crowd surges around me, pushing me forward. "Whoa...?" I say. As soon as the ladies started moving, they bumped into me, forcing me forward, causing me to run right into... SMACK. I literally ran into him. "Oh, I am so sorry," I exclaim as I glance up at his face. He held onto me, almost hugging me and preventing me from falling on my ass.

He flashed a charming smile, his eyes twinkling with amusement rather than annoyance. "No harm done," he said in a deep, smooth voice that resonated through the crowd. "It's not every day I get to rescue someone from a mob." With a gentle nod, he helped me regain my balance, his touch warm and reassuring. The crowd around us held its breath for a moment, watching the unexpected interaction with wide eyes and murmurs of intrigue. Then, as if on cue, they erupted into a chorus of excited chatter and laughter, the buzz of their voices filling the air with renewed energy. People craned their necks to get a better look, their curiosity piqued by the brief but memorable encounter.

After making sure I was okay, he turned and walked away. I watched as he walked away, entering the elevator and disappearing from the lobby and my life. I felt a mix of awe and disbelief as he disappeared. My heart is still racing from the unexpected encounter. Something was captivating about him, a magnetic presence that left me slightly breathless and wishing I had said more. As the elevator doors closed, I realized that moment, fleeting as it was, would linger in my thoughts for a long time. "Oh my god, Sophia... the king held you in his hands. How did he smell?" Jenny asked. Her eyes were wide with excitement, and she clutched my arm as if she couldn't believe what had just happened. "Was he as dreamy up close as he looks from afar?" she asked, practically bouncing on her toes. I could see envy and thrill written all over her face, as if she had just witnessed a movie scene come to life.

"I don't know, Jen. I wasn't paying that close attention to his smell. Everything happened so fast," I replied. I smoothed out my dress before I suddenly heard the unmistakable sound of high heels click-clacking on the marble floor behind me, and I straightened up, knowing I was in for something.

"Excuse me, but what just happened here?" I hear her snap as I turn around to face Lydia Marshall. Her eyes flash with something—envy, perhaps—before she huffs and crosses her arms across her chest, trying to appear superior. "How dare you make such a fool of yourself in front of such a distinguished guest?" she snarls fiercely.

I took a deep breath, trying to keep my composure. "Lydia, it was an accident, and I didn't plan for any of this to happen," I replied calmly. "Besides, it's not every day you meet someone like him, so maybe you could try being understanding."

Lydia crossed her arms, her eyes narrowing as she huffed in disapproval. "Understanding?" she scoffed, her voice dripping with skepticism. "You're lucky you didn't cause a scene worthy of the tabloids," she added, though I could see a flicker of curiosity in her eyes despite her harsh words. Lydia's stern expression softened slightly, though she tried to mask it with a dismissive shrug. "Well, just make sure it doesn't happen again," she muttered, glancing around as if hoping no one else had noticed the commotion. Despite her attempt to appear aloof, it was clear Lydia was intrigued by the encounter, her gaze lingering on me longer than necessary before she turned on her heel and walked away.

02

HIS INTERVENTION

In the middle of checking in a guest, I felt a presence behind me and turned to see Lydia standing there. "I'm punishing you for what you did earlier. I need you to deliver welcome baskets to every floor of the hotel. I'll give you the list of rooms and tell your boss I borrowed you for the day," she says with a snarl. She seemed to enjoy bossing everyone around like this.

"And let me guess, do you want me to do it all by myself?" I asked in annoyance. I knew there would be many rooms with the VIP party starting tonight. As I thought about spending my entire day running around the hotel alone, I felt a knot of frustration tighten in my stomach. The sheer amount of work before me seemed never-ending, and I couldn't help but feel overwhelmed by it.

"Yes, why is that a problem for you?" she asks, crossing her arms across her chest and tapping her foot in irritation. Her dismissive attitude only added to my stress, making me feel even more burdened by the task at hand. Lydia's condescending tone and lack of empathy left me feeling undervalued and unappreciated. It was as if she relished in my discomfort, and that realization fueled my determination to get through the day despite her attempts to make it difficult.

Shaking my head, I responded. "No, not at all. I can handle it." I turned and headed towards the elevator to get to the basement to get the baskets and begin my task. As I walked towards the elevator, I quickly noticed a man and a woman standing in front of it, arguing about something. The woman was wearing a stunning ball gown, and I watched as she hurled a mask at the man in anger. He failed to catch it, and I watched it fall to the floor. "I can't take this anymore. It is over between us, De Rosa! You are a liar and a cheat. I want nothing more from you." She yelled at the man before storming off in a huff. The man, De Rosa, stood frozen for a moment, his face shocked and disbelieving. He glanced around, hoping no one witnessed the outburst, before awkwardly bending down to pick up the fallen mask. His expression softened from anger to regret, and he sighed, running a hand through his hair in frustration.

"Now I don't have a date," he mumbles, glancing around. Our eyes meet for a second before I glance away. Despite the awkward tension, I tried to act cool. "Wait a minute, you just saw the whole thing. Didn't you?" he asked.

I hesitated, unsure of how to respond without making the situation awkward. "Well, it's difficult to miss something like that," I admit with a small shrug. "But don't worry, your secret is safe with me."

"That's good, but I promise I will explain everything to you when we get there." He replied, moving closer to me. I step back. "Aw, please don't do that... don't run away from me," he begs.

"Oh, I'm sorry..." I begin, but before I know it, he grabs me from the waist, pulling me into the now open elevator. I glance up at the man's face as he clutches me tightly. I felt a mix of confusion and concern, unsure of his intentions. His sudden action was both unexpected and unsettling, and I wondered if I had underestimated the situation. As the elevator doors closed, I was keenly aware of the need to remain cautious and assertive in this unexpected encounter.

"Oh boy, I'm sure lucky to find a pretty girl to take her place. There was no way I could go empty-handed... not without a beautiful woman at my side," he says as he glances down at me, tightening his hold even more after I tried to pull away. His words sent a chill down my spine, and a wave of unease washed over me. I felt trapped and objectified, as if I had become nothing more than a prize to parade around. My instincts screamed for me to find a way out of this situation, reminding me that I needed to be careful about how I handled this unexpected predicament.

"Um, where are you heading?" I asked, still trying to break free of his grasp.

"Oh, the ball," he replies to me.

"I'm sorry, Sir. But I work here at the hotel. I can't attend the ball." I tried to explain to him, pushing him away. His smile faltered for a moment, confusion clouding his features as he processed my words. "Wait? You work here?" he asked, loosening his grip slightly to comprehend the situation. Realizing his mistake, he released me completely, an apologetic look crossing his face. "I'm sorry, I'll find someone else." He replies as the elevator doors open, and he walks out to the party. The moment he stepped out, I saw the ball in full swing. The grand ballroom was bathed in warm, golden light, casting an enchanting glow over the elegantly dressed attendees. The air was filled with classical music, mingling with polite conversation and laughter. Guests, adorned in elaborate and lavish gowns, moved gracefully across the dance floor, creating a mesmerizing tapestry of color and movement.

Suddenly, a deep voice came from behind me. "Hello, ma'am... do you have some champagne?" He asked, and I turned around to see a handsome, well-known man. As it turned out, his picture appeared in Vogue magazine this month as America's most eligible bachelor. My heart skipped a beat as I recognized him. His striking features were even more captivating in person. A mix of surprise and disbelief washed over me, and I fumbled for words, my cheeks flushing slightly. "Oh, yes, of course," I replied, quickly composing myself to maintain a professional demeanor despite the unexpected encounter. "You're Zosimo Rossi!" I said with wide eyes.

He glared at me. "Oh, so you know who I am?" he asked. Feeling flustered, I nodded and quickly decided to amend my slip. "Yes, Mr. Rossi, let me get that champagne for you," I said, eager to return to my duties and avoid further awkwardness. As I turned to retrieve a glass, I couldn't help but wonder how this chance meeting might change my evening. Handing him the glass, I smiled and said, "Here you go, Mr. Rossi. Please let me know if there is anything else I can do for you."

"As a matter of fact, there is something. I actually have a special guest I am meeting with. This guest will need some of that special room service that you offer at events like this." He smiled at me, eyeing my body up and down. "For some reason, he loves innocent girls. So you would be just right for him." A chill ran down my spine as the implications of his request sank in. Panic welled up inside me, and my heart raced with a mix of fear and indignation. I couldn't believe the audacity of his suggestion, and a part of me wanted to confront him right then and there. Yet, I knew I had to remain composed, so I took a deep breath, trying to mask the turmoil within.

"I'm sorry, but we don't offer that kind of service here at this hotel," I responded to him and tried to walk away. I wasn't fast enough, and he slipped his arm around my waist, pulling me closer to a table full of guys.

"Do not lie to me, I know for a fact you do offer it here. Especially at events like this one. You're so pretty," he said. A wave of panic surged through me, my heart pounding as I struggled to keep my expression neutral. I felt trapped, the room closing in around me as I searched for a way to defuse the situation without escalating it. I desperately hoped someone would notice and intervene.

"Excuse me, Rossi. But what are you doing with that poor woman? She looks completely scared." I heard a deep growl behind us, and as he turned us around, I quickly noticed it was the king. He glared at the guy who was holding me, making me wonder why. His sharp, piercing eyes fixed on Rossi, exuding authority and power.

"Oh, hey, Morelli. I'm bringing this woman to join me in with some of that special room service the maids offer. Will you join us?" He said with a smirk. My mind raced, caught between disbelief and a desperate need to escape. The king's presence was both a relief and a new source of anxiety. Would he help, or was he in on this too? I felt like I was teetering on the edge of a precipice, unsure of where to turn or who to trust. Yet, in that moment, a flicker of hope sparked within me, hoping that the king's intervention might be my way out of this nightmare.

His expression hardened, his eyes narrowed with disdain and anger. "I do not think you understand, Rossi," he snapped out, his voice cold and authoritative. "This event is for business and pleasure. But not at the expense of someone's dignity and safety. You will release your hold of that woman right now, or I'll be forced to do it for you." The air was thick with tension, as if everyone in the room was holding their breath, waiting to see what would happen next. Conversations around us faltered, and eyes subtly shifted in our direction, drawn to the unfolding confrontation. It felt like the entire room was balanced on a knife's edge, the atmosphere charged with the potential for conflict or resolution.

Rossi hesitated, his knuckles white as he clenched my arm tighter, his jaw grinding with tension. Finally, he flung me away with a muttered curse, his voice tinged with frustration. "Fine, I just wanted to have a bit of fun, all right? I didn't mean to cause any trouble."

03

SOLD AT AUCTION

Turning to me, "Now I suggest you leave," the king mutters angrily at me. I felt a rush of relief mingled with gratitude as I stepped away from Rossi's grasp, my heart still pounding from the intensity of the moment. The king's intervention had not only protected me but also restored a sense of dignity that had been momentarily stripped away. Despite the lingering tension, I managed a small nod of thanks before making my way toward the exit, eager to leave the charged atmosphere behind. I stepped out of the ballroom, my eyes scanning the long, empty hallway for an elevator. Several doors stood ajar, and my gaze lingered on one. Through the narrow opening, I caught a glimpse of something that made my heart stop—stacks of cash, gleaming under the light, with a glint of steel beside them. My breath caught in my throat, and fear gripped me. If anyone saw me now, I knew I wouldn't stand a chance.

Suddenly, someone grabbed my arm and pulled me backwards. I sucked in a deep breath. The man flung me against the wall and placed his hands on both sides of my face, blocking me in. Fear and surprise at what had just happened overwhelmed me, and my heart pounded so loudly that I worried he could hear it. "What the hell are you doing here?" he asked. I glance carefully up to see a tall man with black hair slicked back pinning me to the wall. His sharp green eyes glared at me. He gritted his teeth. The whole thing happened so suddenly that I trembled. *Who was this guy? Was he dangerous? Was he planning to hurt me?*

"I'm sor-"

"No, I don't want to hear it. Just get out of here. You have five seconds to disappear from my sight and forget about what you just saw." He bends down and places his mouth next to my ear. "Because if you don't, I will be forced to kill you. Now, nod if you understand me?" he says, staring into my eyes. Terrified, I nodded quickly, eager to comply. As soon as he released his hold, I sprinted down the hallway, my heart pounding with each step. I knew I needed to disappear.

Once I reached the basement storage room, I took a couple of deep breaths to slow down my racing heart. As I leaned against the cold wall, my mind raced with questions and fear. How had I stumbled into such a dangerous situation, and what kind of world had I glimpsed behind that door? I wondered if I should report what I saw to my boss despite what the man said. However, I settled on forgetting for fear of my safety. I just needed to forget what had happened and get to work. I grabbed one of the empty metal carts and loaded the welcome baskets onto the cart. As I pushed the cart to the elevator... THUD!

I suddenly fell backwards onto the ground at the sudden stop of my cart, and I heard something shatter as it hit the ground. I glanced up to see two large men peering inside a bulky wooden crate. This was dropped on the ground when I ran into it. "Ah man, the statue is broken," the taller of the two said as he ran his hand through his long hair. He looked pretty distressed by what had just happened. I quickly scrambled to my feet, apologizing profusely for my clumsiness. Unsure of what to do, I offered to help them clean up the broken pieces, hoping to avoid further trouble.

"You think an apology is enough here? No, you owe us now!" One of the men said with a snarl. He suddenly reached out and grabbed my arm, dragging me down the hall. I watched in horror as the other took out a phone to make a call.

"We'll see what the boss man says," the guy with the phone says as he dials a number. I watch as he puts the phone up to his ear, and I listen closely to his side of the conversation. As the man spoke on the phone, I quickly scanned my surroundings for any possible escape routes. My eyes landed on a nearby fire exit door, slightly ajar. Remembering the emergency stairwell behind it, I decided to make a run for it the moment they turned their backs. Timing my move with a burst of loud laughter from the man on the phone, I yanked my arm free and dashed towards the door, praying they wouldn't notice until it was too late. The man holding the phone shouted in surprise, dropping it to the floor as he spun around to see me sprinting towards the exit. "Stop her!" He yelled, his voice echoing down the hall. The other man, momentarily stunned, lunged after me, but I had already reached the door and was tumbling through it. The sound of their footsteps and angry shouts faded as I raced up the stairwell, my heart pounding with adrenaline. As I reached the next landing, my foot caught on the edge of a step, sending me sprawling forward. Desperately trying to regain my balance, I felt a hand grasp my arm, followed by another on my shoulder, as the two men finally caught up. Panic surged through me as I struggled against their grip, my mind racing with thoughts of what might happen next.

One of the two guys dragged me back down the stairs. As we entered the office, he flung me into a chair. "Boss wants her to take the statue's place. She is now the finale!" I sat in the chair, my heart pounding with a mix of fear and disbelief. My mind raced as I tried to comprehend the bizarre turn of events, feeling a cold sweat trickle down my back. The room seemed to close in around me, and I struggled to keep my composure, wondering what "taking the statue's place" could possibly mean. The other guy pulls out a pair of handcuffs and clasps my hands behind my back to the chair.

I began to cry when I realized they were being serious and I was going to be auctioned off... *what? Just like that.* Suddenly, a bag was placed over my head, preventing me from seeing anything.

A few hours later...

When the bag is pulled off my head, I blink at the bright light shining in my eyes. My wrist was still clasped tightly in cuffs attached to the metal chair I was sitting on. I was inside what looked like a giant bird cage, and it sat in the middle of a large circular stage. A masked auctioneer gazes at me in both awe and surprise as he says, "And now for our final item of the night, we have a beautiful young woman. You can use her as a toy or keep her for your slave... the options are endless. I will start bidding at $50,000." A murmur of excitement rippled through the crowd, their eyes fixed on me with a mix of curiosity and anticipation. Some whispered to each other, assessing the situation, while others eagerly raised their paddles, ready to participate in the auction. The atmosphere was charged with a sinister energy, and I could feel the weight of their gazes as they appraised me like a prized possession.

As the amount approached $1 million, I searched for any opportunity to break free from this fate. "I have $1 million for her," I heard a gentleman announce, standing up with his paddle high in the air. The auctioneer's eyes widened in surprise, clearly taken aback by the rapid escalation of the bids. He paused for a moment, seemingly processing the unexpected turn of events, before regaining his composure. "Do I hear $1.1 million?" he called out, his voice echoing through the room, eager to see if the stakes would climb even higher.

"$10 million." I heard someone scream out, and the crowd erupted in a frenzy.

The auctioneer's jaw dropped in disbelief, stunned by the astronomical bid. His eyes gleamed with excitement as he realized the dramatic turn of the auction. "Ladies and gentlemen," he declared with renewed enthusiasm, "we have a bid of $10 million!

Do I hear any higher offers?" Panic surged through me, my heart pounding as I grappled with the terrifying reality of my situation. Anger mixed with fear, a burning resentment at being reduced to an object on display for the highest bidder. Desperation clawed at my insides, urging me to find a way out, yet I felt powerless against the faceless crowd that held my fate in their hands.

"I will pay $20 million to close the bid!" I heard a deep voice cut through the crowd.

The auctioneer's eyes widened even further, and his breath caught momentarily as the staggering offer hung in the air. He quickly regained his composure, a smile playing on his lips as he realized the unprecedented climax of the auction. "Sold! For $20 million to the gentleman in the back!" he exclaimed, his voice filled with triumphant disbelief, as the room erupted into applause and murmurs of astonishment. A cold shiver ran down my spine as the final bid sealed my fate. My heart sank, a heavy weight of despair settling in my chest, knowing I was now the possession of an unseen stranger. Helplessness engulfed me, and I struggled to come to terms with the reality that my future was no longer my own.

The cage door was opened, and I glanced over to see one of the guards stepping inside. He grabs my cuffed hands and pulls me out of the cage, dragging me to the edge of the stage. With a firm grip on my arm, the guard leads me down a narrow corridor backstage, away from the audience's prying eyes. As we reached a dimly lit room, I was handed over to a stern-looking man who introduced himself as the buyer's representative. The man led me to the elevator, and I watched as he pushed the elevator button. I realized quickly that I was being taken to the penthouse suite. I became numb. As the elevator ascends, a whirlwind of emotions surges through me. Fear and anxiety intertwined, creating a tight knot in my stomach as I pondered the unknown that awaited me. Each floor we passed felt like a step further away from my old life. A growing sense of dread settled in my chest, leaving me feeling more isolated and powerless than ever before.

04

HIS DEMANDS...

As the elevator doors opened, the man led me inside. He walked me up to a couple of guys seated on a couch in the big room. "Here is the king's prize," he said with a bow. My stomach churned at the word, and every fiber of my being urged me to flee, yet my body betrayed me, frozen in place. The two guys glanced up at me with curious eyes, and upon seeing the guy's face to the left, my heart flipped. "Looks like I caught you after all, princess." He smiled at me before standing up. His demeanor was calm and confident, exuding an air of authority that was impossible to ignore. As he approached, there was a knowing glint in his eyes, as if he relished our reunion. Despite the unsettling circumstances, his presence commanded attention. I couldn't help but feel a mix of apprehension and intrigue under his intense gaze.

"Are you familiar with this woman, Nico?" the one on the right asked. Nico's expression softened slightly, a hint of nostalgia crossing his features as he glanced back at me.

"Yes," he replied, his voice steady and sure. "We've crossed paths before, though under very different circumstances. My boss didn't own her, and now he does." He said, glaring at me with a mischievous expression. It was impossible not to wonder what he was thinking.

"That auction..." The words caught in my throat, my hands trembling. "That auction can't be legal."

Nico chuckled softly, a hint of amusement playing on his lips as he accepted my disbelief. "Legal or not, the world we live in doesn't always follow the rules you're used to," he replied, his tone both teasing and cryptic. His eyes held a glimmer of something deeper, as if he found my naivety endearing, yet he seemed to enjoy the power dynamic that now existed between us.

"Still, I could never imagine that an auction like that would be permitted here in this hotel. Who would have approved..." I asked.

"I did, baby girl." I heard a deep voice interrupt me, and I turned and stared back at the King. He stood leaning in the doorway with his arms folded across his chest. "I pride myself on having the largest auction in these parts, selling the rarest of items," he said with a cruel smirk. My stomach churned at what he said.

"As usual, Drago, you are reckless... this woman isn't worth anything," Nico replied.

Drago chuckled, shrugging off Nico's remark. "Recklessness is what keeps things interesting, don't you think? Besides, value is subjective," he said, his eyes narrowing on me as if assessing my worth. "You never know what hidden treasures lurk beneath the surface."

Nico shook his head, a hint of frustration in his voice. "You're playing a dangerous game, Drago. This isn't just business as usual."

"Maybe I am, but it is my game, and I actually have something perfect in mind for her," Drago replies, keeping his eyes glued to me.

"What plans?" I asked him and immediately regretted opening my mouth.

"Who gave you permission to talk?" Drago asked me coldly. I blink back at him in surprise, my heart pounding in my chest.

"What?"

"Never open your mouth unless I say so," he challenged, glaring into my eyes as he closed the distance between us. "You're in no position to question me," he said, with a sinister edge to his voice. "I have a special role in mind for you—one that requires your cooperation and, perhaps, even your trust." His words hung in the air like a dark promise, leaving me with a mix of dread and curiosity. Nico watched, a wary expression on his face, as if he too was uncertain about what Drago had planned.

I met his gaze steadily, refusing to let him see my fear. "Yeah, okay. I may have been in your stupid auction, and you may or may not have purchased me. But that doesn't give you the right to force me into some role I never asked for." I retorted, my voice steady despite the tremor in my chest. Nico's eyes widened slightly at my defiance, a flicker of admiration crossing his face. He glanced at Drago, gauging his reaction, and then back at me, clearly torn between intervening and staying silent.

"Those are bold words for someone in your position," Drago mused, his lips curling into a sinister smile. "We will see how long that spirit lasts. Come on, I will show you to your room." Part of me screamed to comply, to follow quietly and avoid further provocation, fearing the consequences of defiance. Yet, another part of me clung to my dignity, urging me to fight back, to prove that I was more than just a possession. The battle between fear and resilience was unrelenting, challenging me to find strength in the face of adversity. I stood still, refusing to follow along. "Alright, fine..." I heard him say, turning back around. He closes the distance between us before grabbing onto my wrist and tugging me towards him. I stare at the other men in the room in shock. He picks me up, throws me over his shoulder, and walks away. Panic surged through me as Drago's grip tightened. My heart raced with every step he took. Anger simmered beneath the surface, clashing with helplessness.

“Careful, boss, that girl looks pretty fragile... You don’t want to break her on your first night with her!” Nico laughs and sends a wink my way. I widen my eyes in shock. Wait... that wasn’t what he was doing, was he? I began to kick and scream, determined to prove to him I wasn’t going anywhere without a fight. Fear courses through my veins, but it only fuels my determination to resist. Every kick and scream was a declaration of my unwillingness to be subdued. It was a desperate plea for autonomy in a world that seemed intent on taking it away.

“You can’t do this to me, let me go!” I yelled at his back, banging my hands against it. This was illegal what he was doing, and I didn’t care that he spent a lot of money on me. I’m a free woman. I never should have been auctioned off like that in the first place. I was not his property. “I will call the police!” I threatened.

Drago chuckled darkly and tightened his grip, clearly unfazed by my threat. “Call them if you can,” he taunted me, his voice low and mocking. “But first, you’ll have to get away from me.” When he reached the top of the staircase, he set me down on my feet before grabbing my wrist and dragging me roughly behind him toward a double door at the end of the hall. He opened the door, dragging me into a nicely furnished living room. It looked like a small apartment inside the larger suite. This must be his personal living space. He shoved me down on one of the couches before leaning into my personal space with a smirk. “Now listen up, I have a few rules I expect you to follow. I will take you back to that auction and auction you off to someone else if you misbehave or make me unhappy... do you understand?” He asked, his face an inch from mine. His words sent a shiver down my spine, and I felt a surge of defiance rise within me. How could he be so cold, treating me like a commodity to be traded at will? Despite the fear coursing through me, I vowed to find a way out of this nightmare and reclaim my freedom, no matter what it took.

“Yes,” I whispered.

He stands up and walks to the bar, pouring himself a drink from an unmarked crystal bottle. "That's a good girl," he says, his tone unnervingly calm. "Rule one: You cannot speak unless I first permit you. You are to be seen and not heard." He sips his drink, his gaze unwavering. "Rule two: You cannot talk back to me. Everything I say must be followed without fail." A cold silence stretches between us as he continues. "Rule three: You must answer me with a 'yes' or an 'okay' only."

Inside, I'm torn. Part of me wants to comply, to bide my time and wait for an opportunity to escape. But another part, the part that refuses to be broken, burns with defiance. Every moment of compliance feels like a betrayal of my own self-worth, my autonomy, my spirit.

I was completely at a loss for words, so I simply replied with a "Yes."

"Okay, good. Since you understand me, by all means, take off your clothes," he says without blinking, placing the glass against his lips and gulping down some of the liquid. The request left me feeling horrified, a cold wave of panic washing over me. My mind screamed to resist, to fight back against this degrading command, yet the fear of immediate repercussions rooted me to the spot. I was torn between the instinct to protect myself by complying and the burning desire to stand my ground and refuse his dehumanizing demands.

"What did you just say?" I asked, feeling flushed with his request. My hands trembled slightly, betraying my inner turmoil. My stomach churned with fear and anger, and my knees felt weaker, threatening to buckle under the weight of the situation. Despite the terror that gripped me, I forced myself to maintain eye contact, unwilling to let him see just how deeply his words had shaken me.

He raised an eyebrow, with a smile on his lips, amused by my defiance. "I believe my instructions were clear," he replied, his voice dripping with condescension. His eyes locked on mine, challenging me to comply or face the consequences of standing up to him.

"You can't be serious," I reply, my voice steady despite adrenaline coursing through me. "You just expect me to follow along with this without questions?"

"Oh, I am very serious," he said, his tone icy as he took another sip from his glass. "But feel free to ask your questions. I won't give you another chance."

"What do you want from me?" I asked, trying desperately to understand the motives behind his degrading command.

He leaned back in his chair, a smirk playing at the corners of his mouth as if my question amused him. "What I want," he began, pausing for effect, "is your compliance, your submission." His gaze hardened, the playful demeanor slipping away to reveal a cold, calculating intent.

My heart pounded, every instinct urging me to stay silent. Yet, my anger surged, impossible to suppress. "I won't just stand here and strip like that!" I said, arms folded tightly across my chest.

A flicker of anger flashed in his eyes, quickly masked by calm. He set his glass down with deliberate care, the clink of crystal against wood echoing ominously in the tense silence. "You should reconsider," he said, his voice low and threatening.

05

BUT YOU BELONG TO ME...

"I'm sorry, but I won't do it," I replied, straightening up and standing tall.

Anger flashed in his eyes. "WHAT? DID YOU JUST REFUSE A REQUEST FROM ME?" he raised his voice and stood. "I gave you three rules, rules I expect you to follow as you belong to me now. Take off... Your... Clothes... Now!" he demanded.

A chill ran down my spine as fear and defiance battled within me. My heart raced, pounding in my chest like a drum, but I refused to let him see me waver. Summoning all my courage, I steadied my voice and replied, "No, I will not." His expression darkened, and I could sense the tension in the room thickening. I knew there could be severe repercussions for defying him, possibly even punishment or isolation. Despite the looming threat, I remained resolute, determined to stand my ground and protect my dignity.

He marched up to me, grasping a fistful of my dress in his anger and ripping it open. This revealed my navy blue lace bra. When he saw this, he released his hold and stared down at the hole he had just made in my dress in shock. I scrambled to cover myself. *How dare he do that to me?* "This has gotten out of hand. I am sorry about that. If I ask you to do something, you need to do it right away to avoid angering me again. Always remember that I own you, and I paid a lot of money to own you. Therefore, I am solely responsible for you. "Do you understand?" he shouts before walking away and disappearing into a room before I can respond to his outburst. I stood there, feeling a mix of rage and humiliation, my heart still pounding from the confrontation. My mind raced with thoughts of escape, and I glanced back at the door he had just brought me through. Wondering if I should try it. I grabbed hold of my dress, trying to keep the hole closed, and stepped up to the door, ready to open it, when suddenly it swung open, and Nico and the guy who wanted to take me to the ball both stepped into the room.

"Where do you think you are heading, Princess?" Nico asked as he shoved me back into the room. Nico's demeanor was menacing with a cold, calculating look in his eyes that sent a chill down my spine. "Wait, what happened to your dress? Did the boss do that?" he asked, glancing over at the other guy in surprise. "Maybe he actually likes this woman."

"Oh, leave the poor thing alone, Nico. Morelli owns her now. He can do anything he wants with her," the man known as De Rosa said. I scream when he grabbed my arm and pulled me backwards. "Relax, princess, I'm just taking you to your room." I tried to pull away, but he was too strong. I had no choice but to follow him. The room had a comfortable-looking queen-sized bed, a dresser, a chair, and a small table in the corner of the room next to a bookcase filled with books. "Now, this is the room he has decided to give you. You have a full bathroom over there and a walk-in closet over here," he says, opening a door to show me the large closet. "Now, Mr. Morelli sent Montgomery out to buy you some clothes, and he'll likely be back in a few hours. Make yourself at home, and have a good night." I hear him say before he disappears out the door. I hear the lock click into place. *Damn, they locked me in.* A wave of helplessness washed over me as I stood frozen in the middle of the room; the realization of being trapped was sinking in. Panic fluttered in my chest, but I forced myself to take deep breaths, trying to calm the storm of emotions threatening to overwhelm me. I felt a mix of anger, fear, and determination bubbling beneath the surface. I knew I had to find a way out of this situation.

The next morning...

Opening my eyes, I quickly realized that it wasn't all just a dream. I had been auctioned off, and I am now the property of one of the richest men I've ever met. Fear and anxiety coursed through me as my predicament settled in. I felt a mix of anger and helplessness, knowing I had to navigate this dangerous situation carefully. Despite the luxurious surroundings I found myself in, I longed for freedom and comfort. Sitting up, I spot several bags lined up across the floor and see a note on one of them. As I climb out of bed, I grab the note and read it:

Good morning.

I do apologize as I still don't know your name; however, I intend to find out soon. I sent one of my most trusted men to buy you these clothes. I trust they should all be in your size, as he is the most reliable. At breakfast, I shall reveal my unique plans for you. See you then!

Yours truly,

Drago Morelli

I glanced at the bags. There were probably fifty, and all looked to be designer brands. I decided to put the clothes away and get dressed. Not wanting to upset him on my first day, I chose a stylish forest green lace slim-fitting dress and paired it with a simple pair of black high heels I had found in the bag. It seemed that he believed women only wore heels since that was all he bought for me. Therefore, I guess I would have to get used to wearing them because I never wore heels, as they hurt my feet. Stepping into the bathroom, I brushed my fingers through my hair, trying to tame the flyaway, when I heard the door open and someone walking into the room. "What are you doing, Sophia?" he asked, stepping up to the bathroom door. I turn and look at him.

I looked at him, "What does it look like I'm doing?" I respond with a huff.

Drago raised an eyebrow, a slight smile on his lips as he regarded me with amusement and curiosity. "Feisty, aren't we?" he said, his voice dripping with sarcasm. "I admire your spirit, but I suggest you remember my rules."

"Oh yeah. I'm sorry, but I'm not willing to smile and answer everything with a 'yes' or an 'okay'. So you can kiss that rule bye-bye!" I reply by crossing my arms over my chest.

Drago chuckled softly, his eyes narrowing slightly as he studied me with intrigue and challenge. "You certainly are a breath of fresh air, Sophia," he remarked, his tone both approving and laced with a hint of warning. "But remember, defiance comes with its own consequences."

I maintained my composure, meeting Drago's gaze with unwavering confidence. "I understand that, Drago," I replied calmly but firmly. "But I won't follow orders without question."

"It is good to know. Now I don't know about you, but I am starving. Are you ready for breakfast?" he asked.

"Yes, sure... but tell me something first. How do you know my name?" I ask as he leads the way out of the room.

He smiles at me as he holds the door open. "I did my research, let's leave it at that for now," he responds, showing me the table where he placed two plates full of food. The sight of breakfast surprises me, and my stomach growls in response, reminding me of how long it's been since I last ate. Both of us sat at the table and started eating. "You will give up on any plans you have about running because you have nowhere to run to. I know you have no family. I also called your boss and informed him that you would not return to work, as you are now my fiancée. I also sent Nico to your apartment to get you all you needed. I told him to throw out the rest and turn in your keys to the landlord. You will live here with me from now on, as you are mine." The atmosphere in the room grew tense and suffocating as if the air itself had thickened with his words. My heart raced with disbelief and fear. His calm demeanor contrasted sharply with the turmoil brewing inside me.

"What? You can't be serious? I'm not marrying you!" I replied, blinking in surprise as my mind raced with the words I just heard from his mouth. I took a deep breath, trying to steady my emotions. This was not a situation I had expected to find myself in, and I needed to think carefully about my next move. "Drago, you can't just dictate my life like this," I said, attempting to keep my voice steady. "I deserve the freedom to make my own choices, and I won't be coerced into something against my will."

Drago's expression remained calm, but a flicker of irritation crossed his eyes. He leaned back in his chair, crossing his arms as if carefully weighing his next words. "I admire your spirit," he said slowly, his voice carrying a subtle edge. "But don't mistake my patience. Defy me again, and you'll regret it. If you refuse, things might become complicated," he continued, his tone now laced with a warning. "I'm offering you a comfortable life, but I won't hesitate to ensure my plans are carried out, one way or another." His words sent a chill down my spine, and I realized that defying him could come with risks I wasn't fully prepared to face.

A war rages within me as his words linger in the air. It goes against every fiber of my being to submit to his twisted demands, but the harsh reality of my situation forces me to consider compliance as a temporary solution. Although losing my autonomy terrifies me, the instinct to survive, outwit him, and eventually escape is stronger. It requires all my courage and cunning to appear obedient while secretly plotting my liberation. Finally, I reply, "I understand." His lips curl. Drago's eyes narrow with satisfaction, a glint of triumph flashing across his face. He leans back, clearly savoring the moment, as if he already believes he's won the battle of wills.

06

CAN'T BELIEVE THIS

His smile was colder than his words, sending a chill down my spine. "I've cleared my schedule to take you dress shopping," he said, setting down his fork. "I have to attend the party tonight, and I know you don't have a gown suitable for the occasion. While we're out, you'll need to behave. If you don't, I won't hesitate to punish you. Do you understand?"

I nodded slowly, trying to mask my nervousness with a calm facade. My heart raced at the thought of what this outing could entail, but I knew better than to let my apprehension show. "Yes, I understand," I replied, keeping my voice steady.

As we stepped into the first store, I was surprised to find it completely empty of patrons. It turns out he had called ahead and had the store closed so he could take me shopping. Is he nuts? I was even more surprised at how employees jumped through hoops to keep him happy. I tried on dress after dress to no avail. Drago seemed more dissatisfied than anything. We were at our third store today, and his mood declined. I wasn't sure what he was searching for here, but if we didn't find it soon, I felt he'd send me off, as I wasn't making him happy. As I stood staring at myself in the mirror, wearing my hundredth dress, I silently hoped he liked this one. I was so drained by all the negativity of the day. Stepping out of the dressing room, I am met with. "Yes, that one. That's the dress!" The dress was a deep shade of midnight blue, with intricate lace detailing down the sleeves and hem. It hugged my figure elegantly. The fabric shimmered subtly in the light, creating an aura of sophistication and grace.

After he purchased the gown, he led me to a shoe store and we looked for the right shoes to match the dress. The shoe store had a more relaxed ambiance than the previous boutiques, with soft jazz playing in the background and a leather scent in the air. The staff greeted us warmly, their smiles genuine and inviting, as if sensing Drago's mood shift. Shelves lined with elegant heels and sparkling flats offered a dazzling array of choices, each pair promising to complete the ensemble with elegance. He selected black glitter heels. I immediately thought I would break my neck tonight in those heels. "One last thing," he said, leading me into a jewelry store. "We need the most gorgeous necklace." The jewelry store exuded luxury and refinement, with its plush velvet displays and glistening showcases that sparkled under soft, ambient lighting. The quiet chimes of classical music filled the space, complementing the understated elegance of the surroundings. A friendly associate approached us, their demeanor polished and attentive, ready to help find the appropriate piece to complete the ensemble.

I was surprised when he purchased a beautiful halo sapphire necklace in white gold, as well as matching earrings and a bracelet. I almost fainted when the jeweler told him the price. He was spending so much money on me to sell a total lie. It made me wonder why he was doing all this. Was this extravagant facade meant to impress someone or hide something beneath its surface? Each purchase felt like a carefully constructed piece of a puzzle, designed to showcase perfection while concealing whatever truth lay beneath. I couldn't shake the feeling that this wasn't just about appearances, but rather a strategic move in a game I wasn't fully aware of.

As we returned to the penthouse, he led me straight to his private chambers before placing all of the bags inside my room. "Now I realize we still have a few hours before the party begins. I'm going to call the salon and have them send me their top-notch, most experienced stylist to come and style your hair and do your makeup. I have a phone call to make. We will head downstairs at 6 PM sharp," he announced before disappearing into his room. Since I wasn't sure what to do, I decided to sit and wait on the bed watching the sun set. It was a beautiful sight.

A knock on the door grabs my attention. I stand up as the door opens, and I see a man walking inside, followed by a petite, plump woman. She honestly looks scared as he gives her a nasty look. "Hello, Ma'am, my name is Ivan Montgomery, and I am Drago's assistant. This girl here is Sarah Myers, and she is here to do your hair and makeup. The boss asked me to remind you to be ready at 6 pm sharp. It's a pleasure to meet you, ma'am," he says as he bows before quickly leaving the room, closing the door softly behind him.

"Hello, I'm Sophia," I say as I look at Sarah, who gestures to the bathroom. I follow her into the room and watch as she sets up a stool in front of the mirror, pulling supplies from her bag. She works on my hair before my makeup. She pins my hair back into a pretty updo, finishing with her final touches at 5:35 pm. She quietly packs up and leaves without saying a word to me. I pull the dress on and exit my room, waiting for him in the living area of his chambers. I hear his door open, and he steps into the room wearing a black Armani suit. I slowly turn to face him, keeping my head down as he studies his investment.

"You are stunning, absolutely beautiful!" he says as he cups my chin and forces me to look him in the eyes. "Now for the final touches." He pulls out the jewelry boxes and, stepping around me, clasps the beautiful necklace in place before finishing with the earrings and bracelet. He studies me for a second before smiling, as he pulls a small blue Tiffany Co. box out of one of his suit pockets. "Now this is the absolute final touch, this is what will sell this whole thing to everyone," he said as he opened the box, showing me what was inside. Inside that box sat an extravagant white gold diamond engagement ring. I couldn't help but gasp at the sight of the beautiful ring. He pulls it out of the box and slides it onto my finger with a smug, stupid grin. "I plan on making you into a proper lady, one who actually deserves a man like me." A wave of conflicting emotions washes over me. Part of me feels trapped, like a pawn in his game, while another part is unexpectedly captivated by the brilliance of the ring. Yet, beneath it all, a sense of unease lingers, as if I'm playing a role in a story I never chose.

Walking into the extravagant ballroom felt exhilarating. It was filled with the rich and the famous. I noticed a swarm of women rushing towards us as we entered the room... they had obviously been waiting for Drago to arrive. I watch as one of them tries to push me off his arm. He peels her away without a second glance and tosses her aside like she's nothing to him. "Ladies... Ladies... I already have my date for the evening. Thank you." He cuts them all off, refusing to say anything to them as he leads me away. I glance at their faces as he does and notice that some scowl at me. He glides up to the bar at the back of the room. Leaning down, he whispers into my ear, "So we aren't really here for the party, I really only came down to go to the auction." I watch as he gets the bartender's attention with a single word that he mutters. "Rabbit."

"Hello, Morelli, what can I get you tonight?" the bartender asks as he glares down at me.

"Yes, we want two Broadway Alibis tonight!" Drago says in his usual tone.

"Sure thing, boss, go right this way!" the big guy answers as he opens a hidden door in the wall behind him. He stepped out of the way to let us inside before closing the door behind us. Inside was a simple room with a mirror wall. There were a couple of comfortable couches, and I wondered where we were exactly.

“Welcome, my sweet innocent Sophia, to the rabbit hole,” he says as he touches one of the mirrors, and it slides open, revealing an elevator. He pulls me inside, forcing me to stand next to him, and he pushes the button for the thing to go down. As the elevator went downward, I stood there completely silent, afraid to even utter a word. I jumped when the bell chimed, letting us know we had arrived at our destination. The door opened, and I felt a shiver run down my spine, cringing at the sight in front of me. He brought me to the auction. I was worried that he planned to auction me off again. I feel him leaning down to whisper into my ear, “If you are going to be my wife, you need to get accustomed to coming down here,” he says before leading me along the small hallway to a private box. His words sent a chill through my bones, the weight of his intentions settling heavily on my shoulders. It was clear that being with Drago would mean stepping into a world I barely understood, filled with mystery and danger. I realized that this was more than just an introduction to his life; it was an expectation for me to embrace it, whether I was ready or not.

07

THE ANNOUNCEMENT THAT CHANGED MY LIFE...

"Welcome, Sophia, this is the side of the auction you want to be on." I hear the guy known as De Rosa announce. "I don't ever want to see you or any other female on that stage again... ever!" I smile and nod in his direction.. I wasn't sure if Drago would get upset if I responded to him.

"Hey Morelli, you really shouldn't have so many rules for her to follow." I heard Rossi respond with a sinister smile in my direction. He offers me his chair, and I glance at Drago to see if he cares if I sit down. Drago acted like he hadn't seen the exchange. I stood next to him, watching as the masked auctioneer announced the upcoming item up for sale. It was stock in a well-known business. The auctioneer started the bidding at $10,000. "Hey Morelli, what's next on the list for tonight?" Rossi asked him.

"Nothing you'd want, Rossi," Drago says, glancing at me. "There are several paintings, an autographed picture of Ryan Gosling, a sculpture, and the last item up for bid is a hired hit from the finest hitman money can buy." I glanced away because I didn't want him to read anything in my stare. I watched the auction for a few minutes when suddenly I was yanked down onto his lap. He wrapped his big arms around my waist, securing me in place, causing me to freeze, not knowing what he was up to. I catch my breath as he moves a strand of hair and whispers into my ear. "Relax, Sophia. I am not about to hurt you. Shall we call it a night? You look rather tired," he states, his hot breath sending shivers down my body and goosebumps spreading all over my body. I silently nodded my head, trying to calm my racing heart. I knew I could have easily answered him using my own words, but at that moment, I didn't trust them to come out shaky. He tightens his grip as he stands, setting me down next to him. Then, he tugs at my arm as he pulls me back out towards the elevator to leave the auction.

"Hey Morelli," I hear a deep voice growl out behind us, and Drago stops in his tracks, turning slowly to face the man who called out his name. I noticed he glared coldly at this man as he approached us, which instantly told me he wasn't fond of this man. "I want to say congratulations to you on winning the first human auction yesterday. Can I just say it was a huge success, and some of our patrons are wondering when the next one will be auctioned off?" the guy replies, motioning towards me. Drago instantly pulls me closer to him, holding me tight as if he were suddenly scared that I was about to get ripped away from him.

"She was a one-time thing. I will not sell another person in my auction," Drago announced, nudging me closer to the elevator.

"Hey, boss, is there something wrong here?" I heard a familiar voice ask, and I turned my head to see Rossi standing there with his hands in his pockets. Rossi stood casually, exuding an air of confidence with a slight smirk on his lips. His sharp suit was impeccably tailored, highlighting his broad shoulders and giving him an imposing presence. Despite the tension in the air, his relaxed posture and piercing gaze suggested he was ready for any situation that might arise.

"No, nothing is wrong. You can go back to work." I heard the man reply to Rossi, which confused me even more, as I thought Drago was his boss. Rossi raised an eyebrow, glancing between Drago and the man, trying to gauge the situation. Despite the apparent tension, he maintained his cool demeanor, his smirk never faltering. "Alright then," he said, giving a casual nod before turning on his heel, clearly trusting the men to handle the situation but ready to step in if needed.

You don't realize the problems auctioning her off causes, do you? Did you think everyone would accept this as a one-time thing? What did you anticipate happening? You're dealing with the underworld, and the underworld men want what you have. What do you think they'll do once they find out that you didn't pay any money for her in the winning bid?" he asked through a michevious smile in my direction, and I couldn't help but stare back at the man. Does this mean Drago doesn't own me?

"Listen closely, Mr. Rickman. I make money off auction sales... no one else does. That is the only reason I could do what I did last night. That is without saying that selling her without a profit doesn't mean I didn't pay real money for this girl. Remember that had someone else won that bid, I'd be that much richer? Deciding to proceed without profit does not mean I didn't suffer any real loss as of now, does it? There are so many evil men in this world, men who would totally take advantage of her situation had I allowed someone else to purchase her." Drago said, glancing down at me with a soft smile. I was surprised by his gentleness. "She does, in fact, belong to me, and she will remain the only human to ever be sold at my auction. If anyone complains, you can direct them to me, and I will deal with them. Understand?"

"I understand. I will tell them to back off," he replies.

"You can tell them that the only way I will sell another human being is if that human wants it that way and chooses to be auctioned off willingly?" Drago growls out. His decision to keep me and refuse to sell more humans could lead to significant backlash from the underworld community. His defiance might earn him enemies who dislike his decision.

“Got it,” he replied with a forced smile. “You know Stanley is coming tomorrow. Are you still planning on meeting with him?” he asked.

“Of course I am. It is not as if I truly have a choice now, do I? I have to talk to him about our contract.” Drago says, running his finger softly down my arm, causing goosebumps to spread along my arm.

“Right, well, you know he won’t be happy with this changing direction your life seems to be heading. You know he had his heart set on someone else for you,” the guy says before turning and walking away. Leaving me standing with Drago in confusion, the room felt heavy with tension and uncertainty after his departure. Drago’s gaze remained fixed on me, a mixture of determination and protectiveness in his eyes. I could sense the weight of the decision he had made and the potential consequences it might bring, hanging in the air around us.

“Come now, let’s get out of here,” He says, pulling me roughly into the elevator. As soon as the door closes, he clears his throat, and I glance into his eyes. “What that man said does not change the fact that I still very much own you. Understand?” He growled out. A shiver of fear ran down my spine at his possessive tone, yet there was also an inexplicable sense of safety in his presence. Conflicted emotions swirled within me—resentment at the idea of being owned, but also a strange comfort knowing that he was willing to protect me. My heart raced as I struggled to reconcile these feelings, unsure of what lay ahead in this precarious new reality.

“Y-yes, I understand,” I answer, hating the feeling of being powerless with him.

“That’s a smart girl,” he says sharply. The rest of the elevator ride was spent silently. When it finally chimed, announcing that we had made it to our floor, he pulled me along behind him. We stepped into the small room behind the bar. He wraps his hand around my wrist and pulls me back into the bustling party. "The only people invited to auctions are trusted rich people and the underground elite. The rest of these people have no real clue what really goes on here. They only came for the party." I nod to him, letting him know I heard him, as he grips my hand in his and moves me around, introducing me to a few people in the room. When the party ended, he pulled me towards the lobby. My stomach dropped as I knew what was waiting for me there. All of my co-workers were gathered there, ready to gawk at all the VIPs as they returned from the party to their rooms. With my hand in his, he stepped into the lobby. Sure enough, the media were there, and there seemed to be more of them tonight. "Just stay quiet and walk with me and smile... do not say anything to anyone unless I tell you to," he whispers, and I nod my head. I already knew what he expected of me.

As we walked through the gathered crowd, the constant flashes from the cameras threatened to blind me. But then a face stood out from all the rest. I spotted Jenny standing there with her eyes wide open as she suddenly realized who I was. I tried to send her an innocent smile, but Drago cleared his throat, preparing to talk. "I have an announcement. I want to introduce you to someone who has become very special to me. This woman is Ms. Sophia Quinn, and she is my fiancée!" he exclaims with a smile. Suddenly, flashes erupt in my eyes as he bends down and places a soft, airy kiss on my lips. My lips tingle where his kiss landed. Looking back toward the crowd, my chest aches with panic as I see confusion on many of my co-workers' faces. Jenny, in particular, makes me want to run to her and explain everything, but I can't. When my eyes meet Lydia's, I freeze. Her eyes are filled with fury. She is brimming with anger toward me, and I can't help but wonder why. Why does she hate me so much?

Ignoring all the questions now erupting from the crowd, Drago tugs on my hand, ushering me quietly into the elevator. He climbs in after me. He pushes the button to the top floor. I expected him to stay quiet. "I must say, you did very well tonight, Sophia. But this was merely your trial run," he replies, squeezing my hand harder. "Tomorrow we will meet with a special friend of my father's, and I expect an even better performance," he says, glaring at me. I nod in reply as the elevator chimes, letting us know we have arrived at the penthouse.

08

NOTE TO SELF: DON'T DO IT!

We walk into the main area of the penthouse. I notice that the other guys are all there, having a drink and talking among themselves. But he ignores them and leads me up the stairs into his private space, and I know where I am headed. He flung me onto the couch, the same spot I had landed the night before. I stared up at him, my body tense, as he leaned in, his fingers tightening on my chin. His words were cold, deliberate. "Don't let what that man said about your purchase go to your head. Whether or not I make money from your sale means nothing. I still own you." His hot breath felt suffocating, his grip unyielding. "I could have made money from your sale, but I chose to claim you as my own and forgo the profit. That doesn't change the fact that I own you... You are mine to do with as I please," he said, his voice heavy with control.

My voice trembled as I spoke, the words barely escaping. "And what do you want from me?"

He paused for a moment, a smile on his lips as he considered my question. "What I want," he said slowly, "is for you to understand the depth of your new reality and embrace it." His eyes locked on mine, filled with amusement and challenge, before his mouth met mine with such fierce intensity. A surge of emotions flooded through me, a blend of surprise and exhilaration that left my heart racing. His kiss was both a challenge and an invitation, igniting a fire that I couldn't ignore. Breaking the kiss, he smiled into my eyes. Now head on to bed. Tomorrow is going to be a long day, and you will need all the rest you can get," he says before turning and disappearing into his room.

I stayed where he left me for a minute, sitting there for over an hour. I decided that he wasn't planning to leave his room. I guess he trusted I wouldn't run away from him tonight, but boy, was he wrong. I slowly stand up and cautiously tiptoe back towards the door. I open it and glance outside to see if anyone is there. Seeing no one, I decided it was safe to try to get to the elevator. So I threw the door open and ran down the stairs, two at a time. Once I reached the bottom of the staircase, I ran toward the elevator and pushed the button. I stood there and waited for the elevator to come, glancing around me and hoping no one would come out of their rooms. When the elevator chimed and the doors opened, I gulped air as I realized my mistake. I thought I could escape him, but he was surrounded by guys willing to help him keep me prisoner.

"Where in the hell do you think you are heading?" Nico asks through a smirk, and I widen my eyes at him, frozen in place. Panic surged through my veins as I realized my escape plan had been thwarted. My heart pounded in my chest, and a cold sweat broke out on my forehead. The mixture of fear and frustration was almost overwhelming, leaving me feeling trapped and powerless in the face of Nico's mocking gaze.

I didn't know what to say or do. "I'm sorry..."

"Oh, I bet you are, sweetheart. I wonder if Morelli knows you're down here?" he says, inching forward, causing me to step back. Nico's demeanor was both menacing and playful, his eyes twinkling with a dangerous mix of amusement and authority. He moved with a confident swagger, each step deliberate and calculated, as if savoring the power he held over the situation. His smirk widened as he closed the distance, exuding an aura of control that made it clear he relished the game. I narrow my eyes as he reaches into his pocket, pulling out his cell phone. I watch as he dials a number and places the phone to his ear. "Hey Morelli, I'm wondering if you're missing something?" he asks with a smirk on his face. I listen closely to him as he responds to what he says. "Oh yeah, she's right here at the elevator. You bet, I'll bring her right up." Oh, you are very welcome," he replies as he hangs up the phone, smirking back at me and saying, "Come now, Sophia, you have been a naughty girl. Morelli wants you back upstairs."

I took another step backward as he reached out to grab my wrist. I was so done with everything and dragged everywhere. Without thinking, I turned around and started running away from him... I didn't care where I was heading as long as it was away from him. Glancing back, I hit Zosimo Rossi, who wrapped his arms around my body, securing me there. "Gotcha!" I cried in frustration as he lifted me up from the ground. Tossing me over his shoulder like Drago did on that first night, I just went limp, giving up on running from him. After all, it felt like my only option. Once he was at the top of the stairs, he pulled me through the living area straight into my bedroom. He flung me towards the bed and slammed the door shut without saying a word to me. I sat there staring at the door, wondering what would happen from here. I tried to escape, and Drago knew.

After a few minutes, I glance around the room and notice a few boxes arranged in the corner of the room. I walk up to them to check them out. Opening the one on top, I immediately recognized all my belongings from my apartment. I would be stuck here, and he confirmed that. Straightening up, I began putting everything away, finding new places for my things. When I was done, I surveyed the room around me, deciding it looked okay. I decided to take a long, hot bath. Walking into the bathroom, I turn the water on and wait for the tub to fill up. I take the dress off and slowly climb into the warm, hot water and release a soft sigh. It felt so good. After I had soaked for a bit and felt clean enough, I climbed out of the tub and wrapped a towel around my body. I headed into the bedroom towards my closet, only to stop in my tracks as I saw Drago sitting on my bed. I glared uneasily at him.

He moved so suddenly that I flinched. However, he ignored it as he grabbed hold of my wrist, causing me to gulp down some air as I looked up into his now stormy blue orbs. Why is he holding me like this? He pulls me even closer to him. I could smell his addictive scent. Suddenly, he smiled as he spun me around so quickly. I could barely catch my breath as he shoved me up against the wall, making me squirm as he pressed himself against me. His hard chest against my bare skin and the towel, I freeze as I feel his warm breath run down my neck, sending goosebumps all over my body. I couldn't help but feel scared. I didn't know what he would do to me. I wanted to push him away. I widened my eyes as he grabbed both of my wrists, pinning them securely to the wall, one on each side of my face. "Now, my sweetheart, I believe you owe me something." He whispered into my ear, forcing his breath down my neck. It made my breathing unsteady, and I wonder why he is doing this. "Apologize for running."

"No, I don't owe you anything," I said confidently. He needed to know this was not okay.

"No, huh?" He chuckles, tightening his grip on my wrist. "You see, you are wrong there, sweetheart. You tried to run from me, but there are consequences for your actions. But if you apologize right here, right now... then I might just forgive you," he whispers huskily into my ear before nibbling on the lobe. What did he think he was doing? I nearly let a moan escape as he placed soft kisses along my neck, letting out a gasp as he sucked at the nape of my neck. "Come on, Sophia. What's it going to be?"

I breathe deeply, "I am not apologizing to you. I did nothing wrong. I am a human being... I am not something anyone, especially you, can own." I said confidently.

It was then that he let go of my wrists. Gripping my chin in one of his hands, he forced me to look up at his blue orbs. He had a knowing smirk on his face. "Oh, really now, is that something you should say to the person who paid $25 million for you?" He leaned in, his voice low and confident as he pressed me against the wall. "You will apologize to me, or you're going to face the punishment... what's it going to be, Sophia?"

My pulse raced, and the wall felt cold and unyielding against my back. His lips met mine in a passionate kiss, leaving me breathless. Before I could gather my thoughts, he pulled away, his teeth grazing down my neck and along my collarbone. His mouth lingered there, sucking and licking with an intensity that made my skin tingle. I could feel the marks he left, a mix of pleasure and vulnerability coursing through me. "How about that apology, Sophia?" he whispered, his mouth hovering just above mine.

I stared into his eyes. I wanted to plead with him to stop all of this... because I didn't want this to happen... but my mouth betrayed me when I whispered, "No..." Staring into his darkened, aroused eyes, he smiled down at me before moving to the other side of my neck and immediately began to suck on my skin, only much harder this time. I clenched my teeth together to stop the moan from escaping my mouth. He bit down on my skin so hard it would leave a mark. Ouch... that hurt! I started trying to wiggle free and push him off, but I had no luck as I realized that he was not releasing me anytime soon. He licked at the place he had just bitten, attempting to soothe the raw skin there. I tried to keep my breathing calm and steady, but if I was being honest, it was starting to be more difficult to do. I was getting aroused, and then he began to nibble on my skin as he found my sweet spot, causing me to release a moan that I could not stop. Knowing that he wasn't willing to stop, and realizing that if I didn't do it, I might regret where this was headed in the morning, suddenly blurted out...

"No... I..." My protest crumbled into a sob. "Okay, okay. I apologize. That's what you wanted, right? I'm sorry for trying to run away."

After I spoke those words, he stood up and pulled himself off me. He stood there right in front of me with a look of complete satisfaction on his face. "Do not make it a habit to piss me off. If necessary, I can think of harsher ways to punish you. Privacy is a privilege, and if pushed, I will take it away. Try to run again, and you'll find yourself in my room with me so I can better watch your every move," he says before turning back around and walking out the door. He left me against the wall, breathless and confused. What was that? After a few minutes, I finally peel myself off the wall and walk carefully into the closet. I gather something to wear to bed. I slip on the skimpy lingerie before climbing into my bed. Lying there staring up at the ceiling, I released a long sigh... this was going to drive me crazy. I couldn't believe how easy it was for him to treat me like that. I let my thoughts drift towards him, and eventually, I could feel myself drifting into a restless sleep.

09

MEETING THE MAFIA BOSS

Opening my eyes, I blink at the bright light streaming in from the window. I slowly sit up and glance around the room. I was exhausted, thanks to him. I climbed out of bed and hurried to the closet to grab some clothes and get dressed. I didn't want to be caught in this lingerie by him. I felt a mix of anxiety and determination as I slipped on my clothes, my heart pounding in my chest. Each movement was fueled by a desire to regain control and present a composed exterior. Despite the lingering fatigue, I refused to let him see any vulnerability. I chose a deep violet dress that came to my mid-thighs. The deep violet color symbolized strength and resilience, qualities I desperately needed to channel. It was a bold choice, one that reflected my determination to face the day with confidence. As I smoothed the fabric, I felt a renewed sense of power, ready to confront whatever challenges awaited me.

Stepping into the bathroom, I stared back at my reflection. I was shocked. All over my neck and collarbone were some dark, cleverly placed hickeys for all to see. I tried to apply some makeup to cover the hickeys, but they were so dark that it didn't work.

When I was finally satisfied that they were covered in the best way I could, I turned and waited on the bed. When I hear the door open, I stand up, ready to do whatever he wants me to do today. However, instead of Drago, I see Nico stepping into the small bedroom. When he sees me, a clever smirk appears on his face. "Come, Drago has something he needs to take care of today, so he has asked me to ensure you get some breakfast."

I followed him out to the living area, where two plates sat at the table in the kitchen area. My eyes roamed the room, and sitting on the couch were three large garment boxes. I looked up at Nico in confusion. "What are those?" I asked.

"Drago went shopping this morning and bought three ball gowns. You will need to put them away and choose one to wear to tonight's event. He told me to tell you that you will be meeting a very significant person, so you must be dressed to impress. Each box contains jewelry to match the dress and shoes." I widen my eyes as I stare at the three boxes.

"Wow, okay, thanks," I reply before sitting at the table. Nico sits down across from me and eats. "I want to apologise for attempting to run away last night."

Nico paused, looking at me with surprise and understanding. "You don't need to apologize," he said softly, his tone unexpectedly gentle. "I get it. This world can be overwhelming, and anyone in your position would feel the same. But I wouldn't try it again as Drago has doubled down on security outside the penthouse and hotel lobby. All the security officers in this hotel have your picture with clear instructions not to let you leave the premises." Nico smiles softly. "He's asked all of us to keep an eye on you as well. We were specifically told to do everything in our power to prevent an escape, and none of us will disregard a direct order from the boss!" He explained. A knot of anxiety tightened in my stomach, making it hard to swallow the breakfast in front of me. The realization that my every move was being watched and controlled sent a shiver down my spine, a mix of fear and frustration bubbling beneath the surface. I forced a smile, trying to mask my unease, but inside, the walls felt like they were closing in, my freedom slipping further out of reach with each passing moment.

"Thanks for letting me know, and for this breakfast," I reply, looking at the delicious-looking omelet sitting on the plate with a piece of toast and one each of sausage and bacon.

"Oh, I didn't order this. Drago did it before leaving. I've got to say, though, with everything that's happened, he must really like you. After all, I've never seen him leave any marks on any of his previous girls the way I can see them on your neck there." He smiled mischievously. Ignoring what he said, I ate the omelet silently. Once I was done, I grabbed all three boxes off the couch and returned to my room. Opening the box, I gasped at the beautiful ball gowns inside. One was a deep sapphire, with a low neckline and full skirt. The second one was deep blood red, tight-fitting, and backless. The last one was a black, low-neckline dress with cutouts in the bodice to tease the eye. I carefully laid each gown on the bed, admiring the exquisite craftsmanship and wondering what occasion would demand such elegance. Despite my situation, a part of me couldn't help but feel a flicker of excitement at the thought of wearing them. Determined to make the most of the day, I decided to try on each dress, hoping it might lift my spirits and give me a brief escape from the reality of my confinement.

As the night grew later, I decided to get ready for the evening. I chose the deep sapphire blue dress. The neckline of the dress dipped so low, it showed off my lady bumps very well. I applied more makeup over the hickeys, but I wasn't completely happy as they were still eye-catching. Because tonight's event demanded it, I styled my hair into a delicate updo, leaving the skin there exposed. When I felt ready, I stepped out of my room and stood by the window, staring into the busy city below. I dreamed that I could be one of the many people out there instead of myself. When his door finally opened, I glanced in his direction and released a sigh as he approached me. I stood up so he could see me in the dress. "Oh my Sophia... you look gorgeous tonight. I was hoping you would wear this dress tonight," he announced with a smile. "So tonight I will need you to be on your best behavior. Do not speak unless I tell you to. The guy we will meet today is Stanley Russo. He is the head of the Italian mob and a mean son of a gun. I am currently in negotiations with him about a deal he and my father made while he was alive. This deal is not one that I am happy with, and I am hoping you will help me out of it..." He says as he pats my hand gently. Ever since I became his property, he's been gentle with me, and I wonder why.

We head to the party together. As we stand in the elevator, he grabs my hand and holds it close to him. Inside, a mix of emotions churned within me—fear, anxiety, and a glimmer of hope. Being thrust into the world of organized crime was terrifying, yet there was a strange comfort in his gentle demeanor. Despite the circumstances, I clung to the hope that this evening could somehow change my fate for the better. When the elevator door opened, he led me out into the crowded ballroom. The party was in full swing, and I wondered silently if he would make me go back down the auction hall. We mingled with the guests. He introduced me to so many people as his fiancée. I remained quiet by his side the entire time, talking only when he allowed me to. My face hurt from all the smiling I did. Then, he pulled us to an abrupt stop in front of an older gentleman. "Drago Morelli, it is very pleasant to see you again, son. Tell me, who might this lovely lady be? Is she your arm candy tonight?" he asked with a wink in my direction as if he was trying to be clever.

"Hello, Mr. Russo. It is always a pleasure to see you. This lovely lady is my beautiful fiancée; we actually just got engaged." Drago smiled back at him from ear to ear.. "Sophia, why don't you introduce yourself to Mr. Russo?"

My heart raced as I prepared to speak, my palms sweaty and trembling. A knot of anxiety tightened in my stomach, and my breath shook as I became acutely aware of the importance of this moment. I knew I had to summon my courage, project confidence, and make a strong impression on the powerful mob boss. Taking a deep breath, I extended my hand to Mr. Russo, my voice trembling inside but steady as I said, "Good evening, Mr. Russo." I made sure to maintain eye contact, offering a firm handshake, determined to convey both strength and sincerity.

Mr. Russo's eyes twinkled with amusement as he grasped my hand firmly. His grip was surprisingly gentle for a man of his reputation. "The pleasure is all mine, Sophia," he replied with a charismatic smile. "But Drago can't be engaged to you."

Drago's smile faltered for a brief moment before he quickly regained his composure. With a confident chuckle, he replied, "Mr. Russo, times are changing, and so are we. Sophia is everything I've ever wanted." He wrapped an arm around my waist, pulling me closer as if to solidify his claim. "I realize it is a shock, but I found the one for me in her. I need you to acknowledge that. Could you really deny me what my heart wants?" Drago challenged him.

Mr. Russo's eyes narrowed, and his expression hardened. "Drago, you know this isn't just about you," he retorted sharply. "There are consequences to these choices, and I can't ignore the potential fallout for everyone involved. You have a marriage contract with my daughter, which I must enforce. She flies in tonight."

Drago's face tensed, and a shadow of frustration flickered in his eyes. He took a deep breath, trying to maintain his composure as he processed the weight of Mr. Russo's words. "Mr. Russo, I respect the agreements we have, but my heart belongs to Sophia," he said, his voice firm but laced with a hint of desperation. "There must be a way to resolve this without sacrificing my happiness or yours." Drago glanced at me, his eyes pleading for understanding and support. "Perhaps we can find a solution that honors both our commitments and my love for Sophia," he proposed, his tone pragmatic yet hopeful. "Would you consider a meeting to discuss potential alternatives that could benefit all parties involved?"

10

AN OFFER I COULD DEFINITELY REFUSE

Mr. Russo's eyes softened slightly, though his lips remained pressed into a thin line. He weighed Drago's words carefully. The tension between tradition and personal desire is evident in his furrowed brow. After a moment, he sighed deeply, nodding subtly, acknowledging the complexity of the situation. "Luciana arrives at midnight. Tomorrow I expect you to keep your promise and show her around town. We will meet for dinner to discuss the changes you seek." He replied with a low growl.

Drago's shoulders relaxed as a hint of relief washed over him, though he tried to maintain a composed demeanor. He nodded in agreement, his voice steady as he expressed gratitude. "Thank you, Mr. Russo. I'll make sure Luciana feels welcome and sees the town's charm. In fact, I will bring Sophia with me so that Luciana can get to know her before our dinner meeting." Drago smiles in my direction, not knowing what to do or say, and I simply smile back. The two men talk business, and I just tune them out. I did not need to listen to the ramblings of a man who ran the Mafia and whatever Drago was inside of it. I see Rossi walking up to us.

"Hey, boss, I was wondering if I could steal Ms. Sophia for a dance?" he asked with a genuine smile on his face.

I hesitated for a moment, caught off guard by the sudden invitation. A warm blush crept up my cheeks as I glanced at Drago for approval. "Yeah, sure. Go ahead." Drago growled as Rossi offered me his hand. I took it as he led me away from Drago and Mr. Russo onto the dance floor. It ended up being a slow number, so I tried to maintain some distance between Rossi and me as I was so afraid of what Drago would do to punish me if I got too close to another man, especially in front of this Mafia boss he was currently talking to.

After the dance ended, Drago was suddenly there to escort me away with a deadly look at Zosimo. He wraps his fingers around my wrist and pulls me back out of the party towards the lobby. I could tell he was upset about something. As I followed him, a tall, slim, and charming lady stepped out of the crowd and grabbed my hair, jerking me out of his grasp. "How the hell did you sink your dirty little useless claws into my Drago? I know for a fact he would never look twice at someone like you unless you bewitched him or offered him something he couldn't refuse..." She growled out before lunging at me again. I flinch back with wide eyes, but before she could make contact with me, a pair of familiar broad shoulders steps in the way, blocking her blow. I widen my eyes as I see him standing completely still, unfazed by the blow he just received.

"How dare you attack my fiancée like this... just because I spent one lousy night with you days ago does not mean I belong to you? You were a way to kill the loneliness... until I saw Sophia here. I never believed in love until her... I am not interested in you, so be gone!" he growls out, motioning for one of the hotel security guards to come and remove the woman from his sight.

“Wait... you’re tossing me out? Just like that... but I love you!” she begs, but he ignores her as the guard leads her towards the front door of the lobby. He turns and studies me, glancing all over my body to check for injuries. Besides her pulling a few hairs from my scalp, I was fine. He helps me stand up, and together we climb into the elevator and head to the penthouse he calls home. I was so embarrassed by what had just happened with so many watching. However, I was relieved that he stepped in and took that punch for me. We rode the elevator in silence. As the doors open, I follow him into the main room, where he paces back and forth as if he were deeply in thought.

“Shit, I am so fucked! I didn’t think about this all the way through.” I heard him mutter under his breath. That was when the elevator chimed. Glancing in that direction, I saw the rest of his crew pile into the room. When they spotted Drago, I noticed a worried expression on their faces as they watched him pace.

“Is everything okay, boss?” De Rosa asked, stepping up to him and placing his hand on his shoulder.

“No...” He snaps out, pulling away, continuing to pace. I watch as he runs his hand through his hair and glances at everyone before landing on me. “I just don’t think this is the right idea anymore. I don’t know if I thought it all the way through. I just got so caught up in her innocent look, and thought Mr. Russo would see her and not think twice... but after today, I feel like he might question everything. Fuck!” Drago growls. I just stand frozen in place as I watch Drago closely. He looked completely pissed off, and I didn’t fully understand this.

The crew exchanged uneasy glances, clearly taken aback by Drago’s unexpected confession. Some shifted uncomfortably, while others murmured among themselves, trying to grasp the severity of the situation. De Rosa’s brow furrowed with concern, and he stepped forward, hoping to offer some reassurance amid the growing tension. “Okay, boss, calm down and tell us what is going on? It can’t be that serious!” De Rosa said.

Drago's eyes were wide with frustration and anxiety. His jaw clenched tightly as he tried to steady his breathing. His pacing was frantic, each step echoing his inner turmoil and the weight of the decision he now regretted. Every movement seemed charged with volatile energy, as if he grappled with the enormity of the potential fallout from his miscalculation. "Fine, so Mr. Russo was obviously pissed when I told him about our engagement. He wants us to sit down at dinner tomorrow night and discuss it. But we all know what that means, since the marriage contract between Luciana and I is about to be enforced. But then on our way back here, the last woman I had a fling with literally attacked Sophia, like seriously physically attacked her." He explains with a growl. "She was yelling at her, claiming that I wouldn't look twice at a woman like her... and you know what, she's right! The only reason Sophia is even here is that I purchased her from that auction in an attempt to rescue her," he announces, and my eyes widen at him. He really thought he saved me when he placed that bid. Who knows, maybe he was. However, I couldn't help but feel like he did it all for his own selfish reasons, and I was the one going to pay the price.

"Okay, so what? She got attacked, and tastes change. Tell Mr. Russo the truth: you fell for Sophia at first sight. I doubt very much that he'd stand in the way of true love. After all, Drago, you need to settle down and have a kid, just as your father stated in his will. You might as well make that happen with the woman you so conveniently own." Nico says with a mischievous smile. I narrowed my eyes at him. How dare he suggest that? I'm never planning to have a child for him.

I could feel Drago's gaze burning into me. I turned and locked my eyes on him, and I was met with frustration the minute my eyes met his. It was as if he were fighting a battle with himself. I watched as his smile grew into a grin. Nico says, "Yep, you're right. I need a wife and an heir, and she would be perfect for both." He says before looking at me. "Sophia will be my wife. So I won't be letting her go free after all... let's get started on planning the wedding." He steps slowly up to me, and I stare back at him in disbelief that he will do this to me. What made him think he could make someone marry him? In reality, who am I kidding? As much as it pains me to say it, I remind myself that he owns me. Therefore, he could force me to be with him in that manner. His strong arm wraps around me, lifting me up and holding me against him. He treated me like a prized possession. In a way, I suppose I was. "Sophia, what do you think? Would you like to be my wife and have a child with me?" he says, cupping my chin.

A mixture of fear and disbelief washed over me, my heart pounding in my chest. I felt trapped, as if the walls were closing in, and a chill ran down my spine at the thought of a future I couldn't escape. "You can't be serious," I whisper. I couldn't believe he asked me that. "But, it's not like I have a choice in this matter, do I?" I answered him with a question of my own.

"But you do, Sophia," he said, not taking his eyes off me. "If you agree to become my wife willingly, I will remove all rules from you. I will give you more freedom." It was difficult to keep from pulling away from him.

"You are crazy, Drago, but no. I'm sorry, but I'm not willing to marry you like this." I scream out at him, pulling myself from his grip and running at full speed to the elevator. Once there, I pushed the elevator button to open... but nothing happened. I turn back to Drago and his men. "Let me go now, I don't want this! Please..."

11

WAIT, WHAT?

"You are crazy, Drago, but no. I'm sorry, but I'm not willing to marry you like this." I scream out at him, pulling myself from his grip and running at full speed to the elevator. Once there, I pushed the elevator button to open... but nothing happened. I turn back to Drago and his men. "Let me go now, I don't want this! Please..."

"No, Sophia, I refuse to let you go," Drago says, glaring at me as he slowly closes the distance between us. He bends down and scoops me into his arms as if I weigh nothing at all. He tosses me over his shoulders much like he did that first night, and climbs the stairs up to his private chambers.

"No... You can't do this to me. Let me go, I am a human being! I don't deserve this." I yell out to the others as they stand there watching him cart me away. When we arrived in his private chambers, he walked right past my bedroom into his, where he roughly tossed me onto his bed. I glance up at his face as he suddenly climbs on top of the bed, pinning me down against the mattress. "What are you doing?" I scream at him in sudden fear, trying to wiggle free from his grasp.

"You will stop fighting me, Sophia." He demanded, as he straddled me. I do not like this. "Stop trying to get away from me for a minute and let me explain this to you so you can better understand," he muttered in a soft growl. He slowly released his hold on me and climbed off the bed. He stood next to the bed, watching me closely as I lay on the bed, afraid to move an inch. "It isn't a bad solution to our problem here, Sophia. It makes complete sense for us to marry."

"But I don't want to be forced to marry you all because you purchased me at an illegal auction. Think about it, is it fair to me?" I asked him, a tear falling down my cheek.

Drago's expression softened for a moment, and a flicker of regret crossed his eyes. He sighed deeply, running a hand through his hair to grapple with his inner conflict. "I know it isn't fair," he admitted quietly, his voice losing some of its previous intensity. "But you will become my wife, as I own you, and that is why I bought you in the first place. If you think about it, I will have to find some way to make you mine permanently, or let you go out of the goodness of my heart. And to be frank, I am a pretty selfish guy, so I don't intend to let you go. So, making you my wife makes sense. And eventually, not right away... I will wait for you to want it too, but we will have a child," he says, keeping his voice calm. I widened my eyes at him. It hit me then that he was serious about what he was saying. He never intended to let me go. I was stuck with him forever.

A mix of dread and disbelief washed over me as the reality of my situation sank in. My heart pounded in my chest, and a cold sweat broke out across my skin. The thought of being trapped in this life, bound to a man who bought me like a commodity, filled me with a deep sense of hopelessness. I stay quiet, refusing to look at him, and I glance away out the window into the lights of the city. "I don't want this..." I say, blinking my eyes and letting tears fall down my face.

Drago's jaw tightened, and a shadow of frustration crossed his face, but he tried to maintain his composure. "I get that this is hard for you," he said. His voice strained as he tried to understand. "But I'm hoping, in time, you'll see this as an opportunity rather than a prison. This isn't the way I thought I'd get a wife, but it is better than the alternative. It's obvious you need time to think about things. I will allow you to do just that. I'll be there at my desk working. I want an agreement on our wedding before you walk out that door," he says as he steps away and glides to his desk. I watched as he sat down in his chair and opened his laptop. He gets straight to work as if he isn't just putting me through hell here. I sat up on the spacious bed and glanced around the room. The walls were painted a nice dark grey color, and the furnishings were in whites, creams, and silvers. He had set up an office in an alcove area. It was definitely a room designed especially for him. I didn't understand why he was forcing this on me now. It was as if he was not allowing me to get away from him ever.

"What would you do to me if I refused your proposal completely?" I asked him.

Drago paused, his fingers hovering over the keyboard as he considered my question. His eyes met mine, and for a moment, I saw a flicker of uncertainty in his gaze. But then his expression hardened, and he leaned back in his chair, his voice steady but laced with an underlying intensity. "I hope it doesn't come to that," he replied, a hint of warning in his tone.

"I will find a way to escape!" I announced to him, and heard his soft chuckle as he stood up and slowly closed the distance between us.

"That is where you are wrong, my dear. It seems like it has come to this... we are either going to do this the easy way or the hard way, Sophia. Because, honestly speaking, that is what this boils down to. I own you, remember? I alone decide what we will do, unless, of course, you can pay me back the full $25 million with interest." He growls out. "Since I'm pretty sure you can't, you will have to become my wife. I am willing to let you decide when and where we will say those two amazing words 'I do'."

My heart raced as anger and desperation surged through me. I felt trapped, a mix of fear and defiance swirling within me as I struggled to find a way out of this nightmare. My mind raced with possibilities, but each seemed harder than the last, leaving me feeling cornered and helpless. “Fine, I guess I’m just going to have to agree,” I replied softly. “But tell me something first.”

“What?”

“Tell me the truth, is Luciana the reason you needed a fiancée when you met with Mr. Russo in the first place?” I asked.

“Yes, she is. You see, Mr. Russo and my father drew up a marriage contract between Luciana and me before my father’s death. But I don’t want Luciana. I am not remotely interested in Luciana romantically. But because of Stanley and the deal with my father, I just can’t say no to a mafia boss now, can I?” he says as he inches closer to me. I gulp down some air as he gets closer. He wraps his fingers around my wrist and pulls me into his arms, wrapping them around my waist. Heat emanated from his body and penetrated the dress that I was wearing. I caught my breath as he bent down to meet my mouth, and I stared at his face. The kiss started slow but quickly moved fast and needy. I just couldn’t stop myself from enjoying the kiss, wondering if he really liked me. Why on earth would a guy like him ever want to marry someone like me? When he finally broke the kiss, he stood there holding onto me… holding me tightly to Him. I silently wondered what he was thinking… kissing me like that after telling me I was going to be his wife, whether I liked it or not. He cleared his throat. “I am sorry, Sophia. None of this is your fault. I really should have been a whole lot nicer to you from the beginning,” he admitted softly, looking into my eyes. His eyes were sharp as if they stared into my soul, and I knew he was trying to find forgiveness. I was caught so off guard by everything, I didn’t know what to do or say from here. I could feel him watching me. Suddenly, a sharp tap resounded at the door, and I flinched as he raised his voice to answer the knock. “Come in!”

I glance at the door to see Nico stepping into the room. He raises an eyebrow in his direction, and I break away from Drago, feeling embarrassed at the moment. "Your dinner is served, boss. I had them set it up at the table so whenever the two of you are ready, it is there," he says, glancing back at me. "Um, is everything okay?"

I narrowed my eyes at him. After all, this was all his fault in the first place. It was all his idea for Drago to marry me for real. I have no idea what came over me, but at that moment, I marched over to Nico and punched him straight in the face as hard as I could. As soon as my hand made contact with his face, I heard a small crack, and my hand screamed in pain. I was shocked that it hurt this much, but I stared back at him unwaveringly. He blinked back at me in utter shock, taking a minute to realize what had just happened.

Before he could retaliate against me, I felt myself pulled back. Drago stepped in between us, placing himself between Nico and me. I swear I could hear his silent laugh at what had just occurred. "Why the fuck are you shielding her, Morelli? She just fucking hit me!" I heard him scream, spitting in Drago's face, who refused to move. I shake out my stinging hand as the pain grows stronger. I have never punched someone before. Had I known it would hurt this much, I might not have hit him in the first place.

"She is mine, remember? I will not let you hurt her... she belongs to me?" I heard Drago say. "I will handle her punishment. I won't tolerate another man touching what is mine. She is going through a lot right now. I am sure you can understand that." Drago said, before clearing his throat. "Go and clean yourself up. She didn't do you any real harm. You will heal... now leave."

12

DINNER DATE

Once Nico left, Drago turned his stone-cold eyes to me. "What the hell was that, Sophia?" he asked. I could see anger shining out of his eyes, and I couldn't blame him for being angry at me for what I just did. I acted without a single thought of my safety. I knew Nico was capable of killing me without a single thought, but I couldn't help it. Nico was the reason he wanted to marry me now.

I looked him in the eyes. "I'm sorry," I replied, crossing my arms across my chest. "I'm just so mad. He's the one who told you to marry me in the first place."

Drago's expression softened slightly, though anger didn't completely fade. He took a deep breath, running a hand through his hair as he processed my words. "I get that you're upset, Sophia, but confronting him like that was reckless," he said. His voice was full of frustration and concern. "He was also the one who warned me about you before the auction, and when I realized it was you, I couldn't leave you to those pigs. I had to win that bid, and the only way to guarantee I would win was to bid higher than anyone would dare go." Hearing Drago's admission left me feeling conflicted. A part of me was grateful for his protective instinct, but another part was frustrated by the decisions made without my consent. I felt a mix of anger and relief, unsure of how to navigate the complex emotions swirling inside me.

"Why me? What do you see in me?" I asked so softly that I knew he barely heard me. My voice trembled slightly, and I shifted my weight from one foot to the other, my arms tightening around myself as if to shield against the vulnerability I felt. My eyes flickered down to the floor, unable to hold his gaze for too long, betraying the uncertainty I tried to suppress.

Drago paused, his brow furrowing as he searched for the right words. "Sophia," he finally said, his tone gentler now, "there's something about you that's different, something I can't quite put my finger on. It's like you have this fire inside you that draws me in, and I can't just ignore it." His eyes softened as he spoke, and I could sense the sincerity in his voice, making it harder for me to remain guarded. "You remind me of someone, someone who was very dear to me and whom I lost recently. My little sister died last year. She was so naive and kind to everyone she met. She didn't deserve to die the way she did... it was her death that made me the cold man I am today." He spoke without taking his eyes off me.

Hearing the pain in his voice, I felt a surge of empathy despite my own conflicted feelings. I reached out hesitantly, placing a hand on his arm, offering a silent gesture of comfort. "I'm so sorry, Drago," I whispered, my voice laced with genuine compassion. "I can't imagine how hard that must have been for you."

Drago's eyes softened further as he glanced down at my hand on his arm, a mixture of surprise and gratitude washing over his features. He took a deep breath, as if my simple gesture lifted an unseen weight off his shoulders. "Thank you, Sophia," he replied quietly, his voice tinged with a vulnerability he rarely showed. "It means a lot to hear that from you. Now, can I have your agreement to become my wife?"

My heart skipped a beat as the proposal hung in the air. I hesitated, unsure of what to say, as my eyes searched Drago's expression for any hint of insincerity. "Fine, I will agree to marry you someday." I finally relented.

Drago's eyes widened in surprise, a flicker of hope igniting within them as he processed my words. A smile slowly spread across his face, softening his usually stern features. "You won't regret this, Sophia," he promised, his voice filled with a newfound warmth and determination. "Now, shall we go and eat some dinner? I don't know about you, but I'm starving!" My stomach grumbled loudly as soon as he said it, and I heard him chuckle. "Well, I guess that answers my question!" he says, grabbing hold of my hand and pulling me out to the dinner table to eat.

As we sat down to eat, Drago glanced at me with curiosity. "Why don't you tell me more about your family, Sophia?" he suggested, his tone inviting and genuine. "I'd love to hear about the people who shaped the amazing person you are today."

I felt nostalgia and warmth as I spoke about my family. Memories of laughter-filled evenings and shared stories flood my mind, and I smile. Yet, there was also a tinge of sadness, knowing that those moments were now bittersweet echoes of the past. "My parents both died in a car accident when I was 12 years old. "After that, I moved from house to house in the foster care system. Each home was different, and it wasn't always easy to adjust," I continued. My voice was tinged with resilience and vulnerability. "Some families were kind and supportive, helping me find stability and hope, while others made me feel more like a burden than a family member. Those experiences have taught me a lot about self-reliance and compassion. There was one family, the Martins, who really stood out," I shared, my tone softening with gratitude. "They welcomed me with open arms and treated me like their own daughter. Mrs. Martin used to bake the most delicious cookies every Sunday, and we'd all gather in the kitchen to help. It was in their home that

I first felt a sense of belonging and learned that love could be unconditional."

Drago smiled warmly, nodding in understanding. "It's a wonder how certain people can make such a lasting impact on our lives," he replied. "The way you speak about them shows how much they mean to you."

"They do. I'm still very close to them," I admit.

"Then we shall invite them to our wedding." Drago smiled.

His suggestion took me by surprise, filling me with a surge of joy and gratitude. The thought of having the Martins at our wedding felt like a fitting tribute to the love and support they had shown me. I nodded, feeling overwhelmed by the generosity of his gesture, and whispered, "That would mean the world to me. Tell me more about your sister." I begged him.

Drago's face lit up as he spoke about her. "Layney was so full of life. She had a heart as big as the ocean. She was my rock, supporting me through thick and thin," he said, his voice filled with admiration. "I wish you could have met her; you two would have been fast friends." Drago's expression shifted slightly, a hint of melancholy clouding his eyes. "Her absence leaves a void that no one can truly fill," he confessed softly. "I often find myself wishing she were here to share in the joys and milestones of my life, like our wedding."

I swallowed hard, my voice barely above a whisper. "Tell me, how did she die?"

Drago took a deep breath, his gaze waning as he recalled painful memories. "Layney was involved in a tragic mistake," he began. His voice was tinged with sadness. "It was a rainy night, and Russo's biggest enemy kidnapped her, thinking she was Luciana. Luciana and Layney were best friends. They were always together. That night, they were staying at Stanley's home when his enemy, Alessio Romano, decided to get revenge for something Mr. Russo had done.

Layney and Luciana enjoyed a quiet evening in, unaware of danger outside. They spent the day laughing and reminiscing, completely oblivious to the brewing storm. As the rain poured down, Alessio Romano's men mistakenly identified Layney as Luciana due to their close friendship and frequent time spent together. The night took a dark turn when the men broke into Stanley's home, shattering the peace and safety they had felt just moments before." He explained softly. Drago paused, his eyes reflecting the weight of the past. "In the chaos, Layney was taken, and despite everyone's efforts to find her, it was too late. The ransom demands were met, but she never returned to us. Her loss left a scar on our family that still aches today. The guilt of what happened haunts us, a constant reminder of how fragile life can be. I lost my father months after her death. He never recovered. And don't get me started on Luciana. She was devastated by Layney's disappearance, struggling to cope with overwhelming guilt and grief. She felt responsible, knowing the kidnapping was meant for her, and the burden of that knowledge weighed heavily on her heart. In the months that followed, Luciana withdrew from her social circle. She found it difficult to engage in activities that once brought her joy, as every moment reminded her of the void left by her best friend."

"I see."

"One reason that I can't just walk away from the marriage contract, but I don't love her either," he spoke softly. Drago sighed, contemplating his conflicting emotions. "Luciana and I have shared so much pain, and there's a bond that forms when you go through such a tragedy together," he continued. "But love is complicated, and despite our shared history, I can't force feelings that aren't there. The marriage contract feels like a duty I can't escape, yet my heart longs for something more genuine, something that isn't clouded by past sorrows."

13

MAYBE I SHOULD HAVE STAYED IN BED

Opening my eyes, I stared at the ornate curtains and polished wood, overwhelmed by the unfamiliar luxury surrounding me. Would I ever grow accustomed to this opulence? Could I ever truly love the man who had bought me and bound me to him? Adjusting to this new reality felt like wandering through a maze with no clear path. Each day brought a whirlwind of emotions—uncertainty, frustration, and fleeting moments of unexpected kindness. Finding my own sense of autonomy and peace in a situation I hadn't chosen was a constant struggle. The offer he had made weighed heavily on my mind, keeping me awake all night. The news about his sister and Luciana only added to my unease, making me anxious about meeting her.

Sitting up in bed to the sound of the door opening, I pull my blanket up to cover myself. I stare back at Zosimo Rossi's handsome face as he just smiles down at me. "You seriously punched Nico? You really are a brave girl, aren't you? You know he's killed people for less than that," he says, smiling. I just stared back at him, trying to keep the blanket up to cover the skimpy little nightgown I was wearing.

"Hey, get out!" I screamed at him.

He raised his hands, covering his eyes. "Oh, sorry. I'll leave. I was just asked to come and get you for breakfast. Drago left. He went to fetch your marriage certificate and license," he says, glancing around the room. "Oh, you redecorated here. Looks good."

"Really? So quickly?" I asked in surprise. A wave of anxiety washed over me, twisting my stomach into knots. The thought of everything becoming official made my heart race, a stark reminder of the permanence of my situation. Despite my efforts to remain calm, the realization that my freedom was slipping further away left me feeling trapped and overwhelmed.

"Yeah, he said you agreed to marry him. So he wanted to get things started." Zosimo smiled.

"Got it, but can you leave so I can get dressed?" I ask.

He glances back in my direction briefly. "Yeah, sorry," he says before backing back out the door and closing it softly behind him. I sat there staring at the door for a minute, wondering what was up. What makes him suddenly want the license and certificate?

Without knowing exactly how long I had to get dressed, I climbed out of bed and headed into the closet to pick something out to wear. I grab a simple black dress and slip it on, before slipping my feet into black heels. Heading into the bathroom, I pull my hair back into a messy bun and begin to conceal the fading hickeys on my neck with some makeup. I was still mad that he had marked me in the first place. I glance at my reflection in the mirror and decide I look presentable, and walk out of the room.

Stepping out of my room, I gulped down some air as I quickly noticed all the guys sitting in the living area talking. What the hell was going on in here? I wondered as I looked around the room and found Drago talking to Nico about something in the corner. My stomach immediately did a somersault, and I cringed at the deep blue spot under his eye... Did I really hit him that hard to cause that? Catching sight of me, I hear Drago say, "Well, look who's finally joining us!" I stare over at him in confusion. I thought Zosimos had said he had left. "Come over here, my sweet Sophia, and eat some breakfast. We have quite a day planned for today."

I step cautiously to the table. "Oh, and what are we doing today?" I asked him before sitting down at the table to eat breakfast.

"Luciana arrived late last night, and Mr. Russo asked me to take her out today. I told him that I'd bring you along so that you can get to know Luciana." Drago said with a smug smile on his face. I glared at him as I shoved a bite of the waffle into my mouth. I wasn't feeling up to being his loving fiancée today and taking some girl out on the town; however, I knew I really didn't have a choice in the matter.

"I remember it."

"You will want to change out of that dress and put this outfit on," he says through a devilish smile, holding onto a white cardboard box and shoving it across the table towards me. I glance up at him with confusion on my face, taking the package from him and lifting the lid. In the box sat a pair of designer jeans with a floral print blouse, and underneath the clothes was a pair of pink Vans. I glance up at Drago, eyebrows raised, wondering why he gave me these. "Do you like them?" he asks.

"I do, but why are you giving me these?" I asked, my voice trembling as I held the shoes, caught between confusion and an uneasy sense of gratitude.

"Because you do not want to wear heels out shopping with Luciana, your feet will kill you by the time we are done. I would rather you be comfortable," he says with a smile. "I know Montgomery only bought you heels, as instructed. So I knew you would need these."

“Thank you,” I replied as I finished breakfast. Once done, I rushed back to the room to change. Suddenly, I was looking forward to the day and being able to wear regular shoes. Once I had the jeans, shirt, and shoes on, I looked in the mirror. I appeared innocent and pure, just like he said I did. This made me wonder if that was what he was aiming at. I turn and head out of the room, quickly noticing that all the others have left, leaving only Drago and Nico waiting for me. “Um, where did everyone go?” I ask.

Drago chuckled softly, a mischievous glint in his eyes. “They left to work,” he explained, casually leaning against the doorframe. “Nico here is coming with us as we show Luciana around. I personally hope it will benefit the two of them as they are both in the mafia.”

Nico shrugged, smiling reassuringly. “Don’t worry, we’ll catch up with them later,” he added, motioning for me to follow.

“That outfit looks beautiful on you. You look exactly how I imagined. That outfit was an excellent pick. I will thank Montgomery for it later. Oh, and before we leave, Nico has something to say to you,” he announced.

Nico stepped forward, displaying a serious expression. “I wanted to apologize for the misunderstanding yesterday,” he began, glancing at Drago for support. “I am sorry for disrupting your life the way I have. I understand why you punched me, and I can forgive you for it. I only hope you can forgive me for what I have inadvertently done to you.”

I forced a smile back at him, my knuckles still tingling from the memory. “I... I guess I’m sorry for punching you, Nico.” Drago watched the exchange between Nico and me with a look of satisfaction, clearly pleased that the tension between us was finally easing. He nodded approvingly, giving Nico a pat on the back. “I’m glad to see you two making amends,” he remarked, his voice full of warmth. “It’s important we all get along, especially with everything that’s going on.” Drago then stepped closer and, with gentle tenderness, planted a soft kiss on my lips. I felt a warm blush spread across my cheeks, surprised by the unexpected gesture. "We should get going," Drago suggested, his voice low and soothing. Nico nodded in agreement, and together, we made our way out, ready to face whatever the day had in store for us. The unexpected kiss lingered in my thoughts, a mix of surprise and warmth leaving me slightly flustered. It was a gesture that seemed to signify a deeper connection, a silent promise amidst the chaos of our lives.

14

SWEET TALK

We take the elevator down to the lobby. I missed my days working with my co-workers, joking around, and helping guests. But at the same time, Drago offered me a life of being taken care of, of being pampered and loved. So maybe I should just learn to let my freedom go and be happy to be his girl. After all, there are a lot of women who would kill for a guy like him... and I literally just stumbled upon him.

Drago wrapped his arms around my waist, keeping me close, which made me think he was worried I'd get away. As the door opened to the lobby, I heard a soft, sweet voice sing out. "Oh, Drago, it's so nice to see you again!" I glance out and immediately notice one very important thing here. This woman was absolutely gorgeous. She stood tall and slender with a big smile on her face. She could have been a model. "Oh, Father tells me that you're engaged to a normal girl? What's the story with that?" she says, as she strides right up to him, planting a big kiss right on his lips. I had to look twice to make sure I saw it correctly.

"Yes, I am. Hey Luce! I am happy to see you again. Here, I'd like you to meet my sweet Sophia. She is the woman I am engaged to," he replies with a small wink in my direction. "She has graciously cleared her super busy schedule to meet you and help me take you on a tour of our lovely city."

I watched as she turned and faced me with a curious look on her face. I was completely sure that she was utterly confused as to why someone like Drago Morelli would be so interested in marrying someone as boring and plain as I am. I smile carefully and hold out my hand towards her for a friendly shake. "Hello Luciana, my name is Sophia Quinn. It was very nice to meet you. I hope we can become great friends."

Rolling her eyes towards the ceiling, she reaches out and pulls Drago away for a private conversation. I turn and watch as she runs her fingers across his shirt collar, pretending to fix it. I knew what she was doing. After all, I was a girl. But it wasn't going to make me jealous because, as far as I was concerned, this was all just an act. I was not in love with Drago Morelli, and I really did not want to be here with her at all. I wondered if Luciana's behavior was driven by jealousy or perhaps a lingering affection for Drago. It was possible she saw me as a threat to whatever relationship or connection she believed she had with him. Or maybe she simply enjoyed stirring up drama, testing the waters to see how secure our engagement really was.

"Dude, some of us would rather be at work than standing here watching you get all the attention from these two beautiful women." Nico growls. He winks in my direction. Wait... was he trying to help me out here or something?

I glance up at Drago in time to see the flush in his cheeks as he walks back to me. "Oh, I'm sorry. Luce, I want you to meet Nico Moretti. He's a mafia member here, and he insisted on meeting you today." He says, giving Nico a stern look before stepping to the side and wrapping his arm around my waist, pulling me into his grip. I couldn't help but smile at Luciana as he did it.

I noticed the look she gave me as he released his hold. He then laced his fingers into mine and pulled me out to a limo waiting at the curb. The driver opens the back door, and we all pile in. I quickly notice that Lucianna tries to sit between me and Drago, but he takes the seat across from her, pulling me onto his lap. "I realize that it's hard for you to get used to Luce. But Sophia is the woman I have chosen to be with; she is who I want, so I expect you to respect that and her," he says in his usual cold tone, narrowing his eyes at her.

I see her pout at him. "I'm sorry, Dra, but I can't help but think this Bitch has somehow fooled you. That she could be working for someone to gain your trust. Besides, why on earth would you want a small girl like her when you can have a willing, mature woman like me? She won't be able to satisfy your needs like I can, Drago." She said, batting her lashes at him.

Drago's jaw tightened, and a steely resolve settled over his features. "Luciana," he said, his voice low and measured, "I don't appreciate the accusations you're throwing around without any basis. Sophia has proven her loyalty time and again, and I trust her completely." He shifted slightly, ensuring I was more comfortable on his lap, a clear indication of where his allegiance lay.

Luciana's eyes narrowed, and her smile faltered, replaced by a sharp glare. Her lips pursed as she crossed her arms, clearly not pleased with Drago's unwavering defense of me. The tension in the limo was palpable, and I could sense her frustration simmering beneath the surface. "I will win your heart, Drago Morelli, before I head back to Italy. That is something I can promise you here..." she says, glaring over at me, and I stare at her with wide eyes. Like, really, who does this woman think she is?

The rest of the ride to the first store was spent in silence, except for the occasional pout from Luciana, who disliked being ignored by Drago. I didn't like the woman, but I knew Drago wanted me to be here. This was so she could see the relationship he wanted her to see. The next several hours were spent being dragged from store to store browsing all types of things, but mostly clothing, jewelry, and shoes. "Hey, Dray, do you like this shimmering red dress or the lacey backless black dress better?" she asked, holding two dresses towards him. We were browsing the racks at the fifth store of the day, and I could not help but think that this woman loved spending money. It didn't even seem to matter whose money she spent, as in the third store, I noticed Drago paid for everything she wanted. But he didn't seem to mind at all, so I kept my mouth shut.

"Hmm, well, honestly, I much prefer the red dress more... but isn't black a slimmer color?" He asks her with a smirk. "So in that case, wouldn't the black dress be the better buy?"

"Whatever, I'm getting the red dress!" she says, browsing more.

Drago turns to me, holding a deep purple sheer dress in his hand, and holds it up against my body. "Sophia, I think I want you to try this dress on. I believe it will look stunning on you," he says with a smile. My cheeks burned, not from the compliment, but from the painful reminder that I had no real choice.

I felt a warm blush rise to my cheeks as Drago held the dress against me, his compliment catching me off guard. Despite the tension with Luciana, his genuine smile and thoughtful choice made me feel special. "Alright," I replied softly, unable to suppress a shy smile, "I'll give it a try."

Once I had the dress on and zipped up the back of the dress, I heard his deep voice over the door. "Come out here, Sophia. I want to see the dress on you." I turned to stare at myself in the tiny mirror inside the small room. I thought the dress looked pretty decent on me. But I never knew what he would think. He was always picky about what I wore. Opening the door slowly, I stepped out of the small dressing room. I showed him what I looked like in the stylish dress he had picked. "You are stunning in that dress," he said to one of the employees who was adjacent to him. She was in awe of me. "Yes, we are getting this dress. You have to have it, Sophia. I also want to purchase some shoes to match." I heard him say to the lady who was now approaching me.

"Yes, sir." I hear his answer, and I glance up at him with wide eyes. Never would I have let another man spend money on me like this. But in the short time since I have been pulled into his life, I have learned that he is extremely stubborn. He would buy the dress regardless of how I felt, because he liked the way it looked on me. So I follow the employee as she leads me toward the shoes to find a pair of heels to match the dress. As I slip my foot into a beautiful black glittery heel, I watch as Luciana leans in close to Drago and whispers something in his ear. I watched as a smile slowly crept onto his face, noticing the slight blush on his cheeks. This made me wonder what she had said to him to make him blush like that. I turn to the lady as she clears her throat, and shake my head at her that indeed these were the shoes. I then turn and head back to the changing room to put on my clothes.

Thirty minutes later, I watched as he paid for everything again, including my dress and shoes. She had selected several dresses and several pairs of shoes. After he paid for the purchase, he handed over my bag to me and Luciana's to Nico. He then slipped his hand into mine, pulling me into his arms as he brought his mouth down to meet mine in a long, demanding kiss. I couldn't help but think that all he was doing was performing for her... before breaking the kiss, he smiled down into my face, "Now I think we should grab lunch, what do you say, babygirl? Are you hungry?" he asks, staring into my eyes and leaning his forehead against mine.

15

NO COMPARISON BETWEEN US

"Uh, Drago, why don't you let Sara go now... she's looking tired from all the shopping? Let's go to lunch, just you and me. You can send Nico here with Sara," she says in a sweet tone, winking over at Nico, who glares back at her, looking rather pissed off. Drago clears his throat, with a smile on his face, as he turns to glare at Luciana.

"Oh, I don't know about that, Luce. I think my fiancé here might think you're trying to sneak in and take her man," he says while winking at me as he speaks the words, giving me a light nudge with his hand. I glance up in his direction in confusion before it suddenly dawns on me... he wants me to stand up and fight fire with fire here. But I'd never done it before and wasn't sure where to start.

I muster up some courage and smile sweetly at Luciana. "Well, Drago, if Luce wants to take you out for lunch, she'd better be ready to pay for my shopping spree next time," I forced out, my voice trembling but steady as I added. "Oh, and my name is Sophia, not Sarah!"

Drago bursts out laughing, clearly amused by my unexpected sass. "Well played, Sophia!" he exclaims, wrapping an arm around my shoulders in an affectionate gesture. "I guess Luce will have to think twice before trying to steal me away," he adds, giving Luciana a teasing glance that softens the tension in the air.

I pulled Drago down for a kiss. He leaned in with a grin, meeting my lips softly, and the room relaxed around us. He laced his fingers into mine and pulled me back toward the limo. We all pile in, and this time Luciana doesn't try to sit by Drago. Instead, she sits across from him with her arms folded across her chest, looking pretty pissed off and defeated. At that moment, I felt proud of myself as I watched him tell the driver a restaurant's name, and we headed toward it.

Lunch was pretty uneventful. Luciana and Drago talked about business dealings, and Nico actually attempted to talk to me. But I had a small feeling that he was actually trying to be polite, so I wasn't bored while they spoke shop. After lunch, Drago decided to call it a day with all the shopping and suggested we return to the hotel. "You know, Luciana, we do have a decent pool and hot tub at the hotel. And the VIP ball is taking place tonight. You can be my guest at the event," he says as we jump back into the limo.

Luciana's eyes lit up with surprise and intrigue at Drago's invitation. She quickly masks her initial reaction with a poised smile, nodding graciously. "Oh, that sounds amazing, Drago. I'd love to be your date at tonight's ball event if you're offering. I absolutely love to dance," she replied, her demeanor shifting as if she reconciled with the idea of having him all to herself.

"No, Luciana, why would I ask you out as my date when I already have the perfect date right here?" he smiles at me, pulling me back down onto his lap. "But the two of us would love to take you out dancing tonight, assuming you'll allow us."

Luciana's smile faltered for a brief moment, but she quickly regained her composure. "Well, I suppose I can't turn down an invitation to dance, even if it means sharing the spotlight," she replied with a slight chuckle, masking any disappointment. Her eyes darted between Drago and me, as if assessing the dynamics, before she graciously accepted, "Count me in, then. It'll be an interesting night." The smile that spread on her face made me nervous. The limo arrives at the hotel, and we all climb out, ready to head to our rooms to prepare for our night of dancing.

"We shall meet here in the lobby for dinner and dancing. Does that sound like a plan to everyone?" Drago asks.

"You don't expect me to come along, do you?" Nico asked in annoyance.

"Yes, Nico, I require your presence," Drago smirks back at him.

Nico let out an exaggerated sigh, clearly not thrilled with the idea. He rolled his eyes, but there was a hint of reluctance in his expression, suggesting he knew better than to argue further with Drago. With a resigned shrug, he muttered, "Fine, I'll join you," as he followed us inside.

"Drago, I hope you save a dance for me. After all, you promised me a good time while I was here in California, and you are not upholding your end of that promise at all. Why did you have to go and fall for someone like that? Really, what does that bitch have on you?" she asked in a huff, crossing her arms across her chest. The tension in the air was palpable as her words hung in the space between us. Drago's jaw tightened, and he glanced at me with a flicker of concern in his eyes. Nico, on the other hand, raised an eyebrow and let out a low whistle, clearly taken aback by the audacity of her remark.

I was so tired of the hostility. "Stop calling me names. I have a name. It's Sophia for your information." I responded, shaking with anger. I glanced up at Drago, hoping he'd step in and have my back.

Drago took a deep breath, attempting to maintain his composure in the face of Luciana's outburst. He turned to her with a calm yet firm expression, choosing his words carefully. "Luciana, I understand your feelings, but I won't tolerate disrespect towards Sophia," he said, his voice steady but carrying an undeniable edge of authority.

Luciana's eyes widened in surprise, and her lips pressed into a thin line as she absorbed Drago's words. Her face flushed with a mix of embarrassment and frustration, clearly unaccustomed to being reprimanded. She hesitated for a moment before muttering, "Fine, whatever," and turned away, clearly trying to regain her composure.

Drago turns to me and pulls me closer. "I'm sorry, Sophia. I won't allow her to disrespect you anymore," Drago says with a smile before pulling me along with him towards the elevator. Inside the elevator, the atmosphere was a mix of relief and lingering tension. The enclosed space amplified the silence between us, but Drago's reassuring presence made it feel slightly less oppressive. As the elevator ascended, I leaned against him, feeling grateful for his support amidst the earlier confrontation. "When we get upstairs, I want you to wear the dress I bought you today. We will meet with Mr. Russo for dinner and then take Luciana out dancing afterwards," he explained the plan for the evening.

I nodded, trying to mask my apprehension with a smile. The thought of meeting Mr. Russo made my stomach twist with nerves, but the idea of dancing later with Drago and even Luciana offered a glimmer of excitement. It was a chance to prove myself and perhaps mend the rift, so I resolved to make the most of the evening. As I entered my room, I set the bag down on the bed before glancing out of the window and taking several deep breaths. The city skyline stretched out before me, a tapestry of twinkling lights against the deepening twilight. The horizon was painted in shades of orange and pink, slowly giving way to the indigo of night. Below, the streets bustled with life, cars weaving through the grid of avenues while pedestrians hurried along the sidewalks, their movements a lively dance of urban energy.

Realizing that I needed to get dressed for the evening, I pulled the dress out of the bag and put it on. It looked beautiful on me. It was as if it were made just for me. Standing in front of the mirror, I felt a sense of confidence and elegance envelop me. The dress hugged my figure perfectly, its fabric soft against my skin, and I couldn't help but smile at my reflection. This simple act of wearing something so exquisite lifted my spirits, making me feel more prepared to face the evening's challenges and opportunities.

"Wow, you look amazing, Sophia!" Drago announces as I step out of my room an hour later. "I mean, I almost wish we could just stay here tonight so I could keep you all to myself. But I am afraid I must share you. I cannot wait to see you in white, baby girl." He says softly, stepping closer to me, wrapping his arms around my waist, and pulling me into him. His words sent a warm flush through me, a mix of flattery and comfort that eased some of my lingering anxiety. I appreciated how Drago had a way of making me feel special, even when I was filled with self-doubt. As I rested my head against his chest, I knew that whatever happened during dinner, I wouldn't be facing it alone.

We stepped into the elevator together. The door closed with a soft whoosh as it descended. The gentle hum of the elevator matched our breathing. I found solace in the quiet moment before we faced the bustling evening ahead. As the elevator doors opened, revealing the lobby, I quickly noticed Nico standing there uncomfortably in a suit with his hands in his pockets. He looked completely out of place. Standing next to him was the beautiful Luciana Russo, dressed in a scarlet red slip dress. The slip of her dress reached up to her upper thighs, and she stood there in such a way that she purposefully exposed her skin. At her feet, she wore leather strappy heels and was every man's wet dream come true. Compared to her, I was nothing... a regular Mary Jane trying to be something she wasn't. There was no comparison between us; I couldn't dream of competing with her, as she would win every time.

16

FINE ART OF BULLSHIT

"Oh, Drago, I cannot wait to spend time dancing with you tonight," she says, fluttering her lashes at him, causing me to roll my eyes. This woman and her never-ending attempts at Drago... why wouldn't she just get the hint?

Drago chuckled softly, his eyes glinting with amusement, but he maintained a respectful distance. "Luciana, you always know how to brighten a room," he replied diplomatically, his voice smooth and steady. Despite her advances, he seemed unfazed, deftly navigating the situation with a charm that was both effortless and genuine. As I watched Drago handle Luciana's flirtations with such grace.

We all walk toward the restaurant, Drago holding my hand as always. Suddenly, I'm shoved to the ground. I look up to see him seething with anger, slamming her against the wall, his hand around her throat. "What the hell do you think you're doing, Luciana?" he growls, teeth clenched. "You don't get to harm what's mine!" Heat floods my cheeks as the lobby falls silent, every eye fixed on us. My body trembles, caught between fury and humiliation.

"Hey, boss, think about what you are doing. There are many witnesses." Nico says as he glances around the crowded lobby.

I stand up, smoothing my dress, and approach Drago, gently placing my hand on his arm to guide him away from her. "Drago," I whisper, my voice trembling as I grip his arm. "I'm okay. Please, let's just go meet Mr. Russo. We can dance, or we can call it a night. Just... please, stop."

Drago's eyes softened as he met my gaze, the storm of anger in them gradually subsiding. He took a deep breath, releasing his grip on Luciana and stepping back, his posture relaxing slightly. "Alright," he murmured, wrapping an arm around my shoulders protectively, "let's focus on what's important tonight." As we walked to the restaurant, I glanced at Luciana and noticed Nico walking closely by her side. Drago approached the hostess. "Morelli, I have a reservation for a private room."

The girl smiled back at him. "Yes, sir, right this way. Some of your group have already arrived," she said, turning to lead the way through the tables into the private room. The private room was elegantly decorated, with dim lighting casting a warm glow over the polished wooden table set for a feast. Soft jazz music played in the background, creating an intimate and sophisticated ambiance. The scent of freshly baked bread and rich Italian spices wafted through the air, adding to the inviting atmosphere as we settled into our seats. At the table sat Mr. Russo with two big men on each side of him, as if they were his personal bodyguards. Mr. Russo exuded an air of quiet authority, his sharp eyes observing everything with a keen intelligence. He was impeccably dressed in a tailored suit, the dark fabric contrasting with his silver hair, which was slicked back with precision. Despite his calm exterior, there was an underlying intensity in his gaze that commanded respect and attention from everyone in the room.

"Good of you to finally arrive. What happened to punctuality?" Mr. Russo demanded.

Drago offered a polite smile, his earlier tension replaced by a calm demeanor. “Apologies, Mr. Russo,” he replied smoothly, “we encountered a slight delay, but we’re here now and ready for business.” Luciana, on the other hand, seemed slightly flustered, avoiding direct eye contact as she murmured a soft apology, her fingers nervously twisting the fabric of her dress.

“What’s the matter, Dove?” Mr. Russo asked Luciana with concern.

Luciana’s eyes flickered up to meet Mr. Russo’s, a faint blush coloring her cheeks as she tried to compose herself. “Daddy, it’s nothing. Just a bit flustered, I guess,” she admitted with a small, wavering smile. Her voice was barely above a whisper, but there was sincerity in her tone that reassured Mr. Russo, who nodded understandingly.

“Why, what do you have to be flustered about?” he demanded of her.

Drago quickly interjected, hoping to ease the tension. “I think it’s just the anticipation of the evening’s discussions, Mr. Russo,” he offered, glancing reassuringly at Luciana. “We’ve all been looking forward to this meeting, and sometimes the excitement can be a bit overwhelming.”

“That may be so,” Mr. Russo says, scrutinizing Drago as he looks at his daughter. “Especially since I’m not going to be able to bless this union of yours, Drago.” A tense silence descended over the room, the air thick with unspoken emotions. Luciana’s face fell, her earlier blush replaced by a pale unease, while Drago’s calm facade slipped slightly, a hint of frustration flickering in his eyes. The bodyguards exchanged wary glances, their stoic expressions betraying a momentary surprise at Mr. Russo’s unexpected declaration.

Drago took a deep breath, his jaw clenching as he struggled to maintain his composure. “Mr. Russo, with all due respect, your blessing was never a requirement for our happiness,” he replied, his voice steady but laced with simmering intensity. “I didn’t ask for permission. I just want to get out of the contract, and I believe we can come to acceptable terms benefiting both of us.”

Mr. Russo leaned back in his chair, his eyes narrowing as he considered Drago’s words. “The contract was put in place to ensure stability and mutual benefit for both families,” he explained, his voice carrying a weight of authority. “It’s not just about personal happiness; it’s about preserving alliances and securing the future for everyone involved.”

Drago nodded, understanding the situation. “Perhaps there’s a way to amend the terms so that both families can still benefit without binding us to an unwanted future,” he suggested thoughtfully. “Maybe we could explore joint ventures or partnerships that align with both of our interests, ensuring prosperity without the marriage contract?” “By focusing on business collaborations, we could strengthen our families’ economic ties and create new growth opportunities,” Drago proposed. “Joint ventures could lead to shared innovations and market expansion, benefitting everyone involved. This way, we can maintain the alliance’s spirit while allowing Luciana and I to pursue our own paths.”

Mr. Russo’s face turned crimson as he slammed his fist on the table, his voice rising with indignation. “How dare you suggest such a thing? Our families have upheld this tradition for generations, and you think a mere business collaboration can replace the sanctity of marriage?” he bellowed, glaring at Drago with fiery eyes. “There are parts of the contract that must be upheld. How would Luciana birth a Morelli child, without this marriage?”

Drago remained calm, gathering his thoughts. “What do you mean, birth a Morelli child? If I’m not married to her, she’ll have one of her husband’s children.”

“In the contract, it states that you will have a child together. If you’re not with her, how will that part be fulfilled?” Mr. Russo’s words struck me like a cold, hard blow. The thought of Lucianna’s future, her very being reduced to a mere transaction, made me feel physically ill.

Drago took a deep breath, trying to comprehend the full implications. "So, you're saying that the contract explicitly requires Luciana and me to have a child together, regardless of whether we remain married?" he asked, seeking confirmation.

Mr. Russo nodded gravely, emphasizing the obligation's seriousness. "This clause was included to ensure the continuation of our bloodlines and solidify our alliance through lineage," he explained, leaving Drago pondering the weight of tradition versus personal freedom.

Drago's heart sank as he realized the contract's impact on Luciana's autonomy. "But what about Luciana's choice in all this?" he questioned, concerned for her agency and future. "Surely, she should have the right to decide when and with whom she wants to have children, without being bound by outdated expectations."

"I want to be with you, Drago. I thought I'd made that clear enough today!" I hear Luciana say and glance at her to see her wink at him.

"But I want Sophia," Drago replied, his voice tinged with frustration. My heart skipped a beat at his words, yet doubt crept in just as quickly. Did he truly mean it, or was this another act for Russo? "She has my heart, and it's not something I can easily change. This isn't just about expectations; it's about what feels right for me, too."

Not wanting to hear more of the conversation, I stand to leave to go to the restroom. "Where are you heading, my child?" Mr. Russo asks. He nods to the man on his left, who nods back to him.

"The bathroom," I replied, stepping away from the table. Once inside the room, I stared at my reflection in the mirror. I started to question whether or not Drago was speaking the truth about me having his heart. A mix of doubt and hope swirled within me, leaving me uncertain about his sincerity. Was he truly torn between duty and love, or was this just another layer of the intricate game being played? As I gazed into my own eyes, I couldn't help but wonder if I dared to trust his words, or if I was merely setting myself up for heartache.

17

THIS MEANS WAR

I take a deep breath and step out of the bathroom and back into the restaurant. I catch sight of Drago when two powerful and bulky arms wrap around my body, pulling me against a strong chest. I try to scream, but the guy covers my mouth quickly, cutting off my attempt. "I wouldn't do that if I were you. Love!" I hear him say as he holds a white cloth over my mouth and nose, and the sweet smell of chemicals swarms through my senses. My eyes grow heavy, and the people around me begin to blur as I struggle to keep my lids open.

Several hours later...

As I blink my eyes open, I realize I am indeed in trouble. What was I going to do? The room is dimly lit, with only a small, flickering bulb hanging from the ceiling, casting eerie shadows on the cold, concrete walls. The air is thick and musty, and the faint sound of dripping water echoes in the distance. As my vision clears, I notice a single, barred window high up on the wall, revealing nothing but darkness outside. A figure steps into the light, revealing a face I recognize well- Luciana. "Surprised to see me?" she smirks, her voice dripping with malice. “I’ve been waiting for this moment for a long time, and now you’re finally within my grasp.”

“You won’t get away with this!” I tell her.

Luciana laughed coldly, her eyes glinting with dangerous intensity. “Oh, but I already have,” she replied, moving closer. “You see, I just needed to get you out of the way. He’ll forget about you. All I need to do is keep you out of his sight, and he’ll fall back in love with me. I just know it.”

“You really are crazy, you know that? What makes you think he’ll forget me? Maybe he’ll move mountains to find me, and when he does, you’ll have to kiss any possibility of a relationship, big or small, bye-bye,” I reply with gritted teeth, trying to break free from the ropes I was bound by.

Luciana’s face was twisted with desperation and determination. “You don’t understand,” she hissed. “I’ve loved him since I met him, and I’ve been there when he lost his sister. She was my best friend, too. He was there for me, and I loved him more for it. And you just showed up, and now he wants someone else?” She paused, her voice softening with a hint of vulnerability. “This is my chance to finally have the life I always dreamed of, and I’m not willing to let you stand in my way.” Fear and anger churned inside me as I listened to Luciana’s confession. I couldn’t believe how far she was willing to go to pursue her twisted idea of love. Despite the panic rising within me, I knew I had to stay calm and think of a way to escape this nightmare. Her words echoed in my mind, revealing a depth of obsession that was both unsettling and pitiable. I couldn’t help but wonder how love could become so distorted, turning a friend into an enemy. Despite the gravity of my situation, I felt a pang of sympathy for Luciana, understanding that her actions stemmed from a place of deep hurt and longing.

“I understand the hurt you must have suffered through losing her, but have you ever stopped to think that maybe it is because of her that he doesn’t see you that way?” I asked.

Luciana's expression faltered for a moment, her eyes flickering with uncertainty. Her fierce determination wavered as she processed the question, the reality of my words slowly sinking in. Yet, as quickly as the vulnerability appeared, it vanished, replaced by a steely resolve. "Okay... fine, I've had enough. Boys..."

"Yes, Mrs. Russo?" I heard a deep voice reply and saw two bulky men approaching her, glaring at me. One of the guys put his hand in his pocket and... wait, is he going to pull out a gun? My entire body freezes at the thought. I knew at that moment that I needed to leave here somehow. I needed to escape. I couldn't take my eyes off the guy with his hand in his pocket... what should I do now?

Suddenly, the door bursts open, and Drago charges in, his face a mix of fury and determination. "Luciana, your obsession ends here," he declares, stepping between us. Luciana's smug expression falters, and she takes a step back, realizing her plan is unraveling. "I won't let you hurt her," Drago continues, his gaze fixed on her with unwavering resolve.

"What? Drago... and Nico. What are you doing here?" Luciana screeches out as Nico charges at her, knocking her to the ground. I watch in horror as Drago takes the big guy and pulls out a gun, pointing it at him, and Drago freezes. The room is thick with tension, every muscle in Drago's body coiled like a spring ready to snap. The men exchange glances, their bravado faltering as they assess the situation. Drago's unwavering gaze and the glint of the gun make it clear that he would not back down, creating a silent standoff that hangs heavily in the air. In a moment of tense silence, Luciana weighs her options, her mind racing as she realizes the gravity of her predicament.

Sensing her hesitation, Drago asserts his authority, his voice calm but firm. "Let's end this peacefully, Luciana. You can walk away now, or we can all face consequences that none of us want." The room feels charged, each second ticking with anticipation until Luciana finally lowers her gaze, signaling her surrender. "Think about it, Luciana," Drago continues, his voice steady, "if you push this any further, it won't just be us in this room who suffer. The authorities will get involved, and you know they won't overlook what's happened here." He pauses, letting the weight of his words sink in, "You could lose everything—your freedom, your reputation, everything you've worked for. Is that a risk you're willing to take?"

"I-I'm sorry, Drago." She says. "Drop the gun, Carlos." Carlos hesitates, his grip on the gun tightening as he glances uncertainly between Luciana and Drago. The conflict is clear on his face; loyalty to Luciana battles with the fear of the consequences Drago has laid out. Finally, with a resigned sigh, he lowers the weapon, acknowledging the inevitable outcome.

Nico steps up to me and unties the rope. "Leave. I don't want to see your face right now, Luciana. I will discuss what happened here with your father. You're lucky she's unharmed." He growled at her. Luciana's eyes well up with tears, relief and shame washing over her. Her shoulders slump as the weight of her choices hits her, and she nods silently, acknowledging the gravity of the situation.

"That woman sure is lucky that's all you'll do." I hear Nico say, as I silently watch her and her two goons leave.

"Right, had she been hurt, this would have ended a whole lot differently," Drago says, wrapping his arm around my waist, pulling me into a tight hug. "It's a good thing I put that GPS tracking app on your phone."

"You did what?" I asked.

Drago chuckled softly, his tone both apologetic and protective. "I know it sounds invasive, but it was for your safety. I couldn't take any chances knowing the kind of people we're dealing with." His eyes softened as he looked at me, "It might have been the only reason we found you in time." I felt a mix of relief and disbelief that it was all finally over. My heart was still pounding from the adrenaline, but the warmth of Drago's embrace helped to calm my nerves. Despite the invasion of privacy, I couldn't help but be grateful for his protective instincts that might have saved my life.

"Now come, let us get home." He dragged me out of the room. We walked through the dimly lit corridors, our footsteps breaking the silence. Once outside, the cool night air greeted us, a stark contrast to the tense atmosphere we had just left behind. As we drove home, the city lights whizzed by, each passing moment a step further from the chaos, and closer to the safety and comfort of the hotel he called home.

As the limo pulled up to the curb, my heart raced. I wasn't sure why, but I suddenly felt nervous like something bad was about to happen. Trying to ease my mind, I follow Drago out of the vehicle. Suddenly, I hear footsteps coming from every direction."What the hell is going on now?" I hear Nico raise his voice, and I glance around us only to realize we were surrounded on all sides by men dressed in black suits. Drago's eyes narrowed as he assessed the situation, his protective instincts kicking in immediately. He positioned himself in front of me, shielding me from any potential threat, his body tense and ready for action. "Stay close," he whispered urgently, his voice calm but firm, as he scanned the crowd, trying to gauge their intentions and formulate a plan of escape.

Then I saw him, Mr. Russo, standing at the top of the stairwell, his hands on his hips and glaring down at Drago. "My daughter told me about what happened tonight, and I am here to let you know that I refuse to renegotiate the terms of the contract. Drago, you will marry Luciana. I've decided that the wedding will take place in the morning." He laughed and commanded, "Boys, get the girl!" The words hit me like a blow, my heart sinking as my knees trembled. The world seemed to spin, and a wave of nausea swept over me, bile rising in my throat.

Drago's jaw clenched, and his eyes blazed with defiance as he faced Mr. Russo. "Over my dead body," he growled, his voice low and dangerous. He shifted slightly, preparing himself for a fight, ready to protect me at all costs. The men in black suits advanced, their intentions clear as they moved to surround us more tightly. Drago didn't hesitate, launching into action with swift, precise movements, taking down the first two men with calculated strikes. I watched in awe and fear, my heart pounding, as the chaos unfolded around us. Drago fought fiercely, his determination and skill holding the attackers at bay as he worked to keep us safe. When he realized he was outnumbered, he turned to me, his voice sharp and urgent. “Run, Sophia. Get to the penthouse and hide.” I wanted to protest, my chest tightening at the thought of leaving him, but his eyes were unwavering, filled with a certainty that pushed me into action. My legs moved before I could even process the decision, my heart heavy with the weight of his command.

18

GETTING AWAY

Panic surged through me at the thought of leaving him behind, but I knew I had to trust his judgment. My heart ached with worry and fear for Drago's safety, yet a surge of determination propelled me forward as I turned to flee. With each step, I battled the instinct to look back, knowing that my best chance of helping him was to follow his command.

After reaching the elevator, I push the button and pray that it will come before anyone reaches me. "Sophia? What's wrong?" I heard the question and glanced at one of my old co-workers who was standing there. I was out of breath. I knew something was wrong, so I pointed towards the door where two big men burst through.

"Call security!" I gasp, my voice urgent and strained. "Men are attacking Drago, and they're coming this way." My coworker's eyes widen in alarm, and without wasting another second, he pulls out his phone to alert the authorities. As I glanced back towards the elevator, I wished it to arrive faster, each second feeling like an eternity. The distant ding of the elevator echoed like a lifeline amidst the chaos, but the doors seemed to open in agonizing slow motion. My pulse raced, each heartbeat drumming louder as the footsteps of the attackers grew closer. As the doors finally slid apart, I leaped inside, frantically pressing the button for the penthouse while casting one last desperate look towards the entrance, hoping Drago would somehow appear unscathed. As the elevator chimed announcing my arrival, I stepped into the main room of the penthouse as the doors opened, only to find it completely empty. I rushed up the stairs to my room in a panic. I didn't have any idea how to lock the elevator, so I knew those guys would find their way up here eventually. I needed to hide from everyone since no one was here to help. After opening the door to my room, I heard the elevator chime. This let me know that someone had arrived in the penthouse. Not knowing who the person was, I rushed inside, scanning the room for a place to hide. Somewhere they wouldn't think to look, somewhere I could feel safe. Not seeing any place better, I dove under the bed and remained as quiet as I could.

I saw the bedroom door open and noticed a pair of feet entering the room. They were wearing black Italian loafers, so I knew it had to be one of the guys sent to chase after me. I covered my mouth with my hand and tried to control my breathing. My eyes were fixed on those shoes as they walked through my room. Suddenly, they stopped, and I watched in horror as the man got down on all fours to look under the bed. I screamed as he pulled me out of my hiding spot by my ankle. He grabbed me quickly, engulfing me in his arms, and placed his hand on my mouth to keep me quiet. "Relax girl, I will not harm you. My orders are simply to take you to Mr. Russo," he said with an Italian accent.

"Think again, Asshole. I will not allow you to leave with my boss's girl." I hear a deep voice boom through the room. I glance over and see Zosimos Rossi standing in the doorway with a gun in his hand, pointed right at the man. I watch as Rossi releases the safety. "Would you mind telling me why you are here and why you are after her?" he growls out, teeth clenched, finger on the trigger.

The man holding me hesitated, his grip loosening slightly. "Mr. Russo wants her for leverage against your boss," he replied, his voice shaky but defiant.

Rossi narrowed his eyes, his finger twitching on the trigger. "Leverage or not, you won't leave with her today," Rossi declared, his voice icy. "Now let her go, or you'll find out how serious I am." The moment the guy released his hold of me, I ran to Rossi, standing behind him. "Now, I suggest you go and tell your boss you couldn't find her." The man's face turned pale as he realized the gravity of the situation. His bravado faded, replaced by a mix of fear and uncertainty. With a reluctant nod, he slowly backed away, hands raised in surrender, before quickly retreating from the room. "You're safe now, Sophia."

"Come here, Sophia." I hear a deep voice order from the main room, and I widen my eyes at Zosimo. But as the two of us stepped into the room, I relaxed as Nico was the only person in the room.

"Wait, how are you here? Where is Drago?" I asked.

"Drago is still downstairs. It's not looking good." Nico admits. "He's trying to hold off Russo's men, but he's outnumbered," Nico continued, a concern etched on his face. "We need to figure out how to get out of here safely before they overpower him." Rossi nodded, his expression grim. "Drago has ordered me to get Sophia out of here."

"We'll take the secret passage through the old wine cellar," Rossi suggested. "It's hidden well enough to avoid detection, and it leads to the street behind the building."

Nico nodded in agreement, adding, "I'll create a diversion to draw Russo's men away, giving you both a clear path to escape."

"Wait, I want to know what is going on here? Why is Mr. Russo after me?" I asked. I wanted answers, and I wasn't following along anymore until I got them.

"Because Drago isn't willing to back down and marry Luciana. If I'm being honest here, I think the man might actually be falling for you, my dear. He's pretty sure about his decision to marry you. This contract was drawn up shortly before his father died. If I'm being honest, I think it was Luciana and Mr. Russo who forced him to and then killed him. Because right after the funeral, Mr. Russo pulled Drago to the side and showed him the contract. Then he read the will, which said something completely different."

"What did the will say?" I asked, interested in the answer.

"Drago's father always understood Drago wanted to marry for love. He was supportive of that. But Mr. Russo had other ideas and demanded a marriage contract between Luciana and Drago. This was merely because Drago, in a weak state, slept with Luciana and took her virginity. After that night, she swore to love him and want only Drago. But Drago realized it was a mistake, and has pushed her away ever since. Or tried to." Rossi explained to me. "Now come on. We don't have much time. I can explain more once we are away from the hotel. We need to act swiftly and cautiously," Rossi urged, glancing around nervously. "There's more at stake here than just a contract. Lives and legacies are intertwined, and Drago's freedom—perhaps even his safety—depends on what we do next."

I silently follow him out the door, towards the elevator. "Once you get to the wine cellar in the basement, take her to the airport. I have my private plane ready to take her to a safe house. I need to find one somewhere Mr. Russo would never think to look. Rossi, I want you to go with her and protect her with your life." Nico says as the door slides open. I glance up before they close to see that he has his phone to his ear and is issuing orders. As the elevator descends, I can't shake the weight of Nico's words. The urgency in his voice and Rossi's nervous glances make it clear—this situation is far more dangerous than I realized. Every second counts, and the stakes couldn't be higher.

"What's a safe house? Rossi?" I asked.

He scoffed at me. "You really don't know what a safe house is?" he laughed. "It's a secure location where someone can hide from danger," he explained, his tone serious. "We use them to protect people when their safety is at risk. And trust me, in this situation, a safe house might be the only thing that'll keep you alive."

As the elevator doors opened, I quickly noticed that we were in the basement. I followed him down the hallway, passing the storage room. I had a brief run-in with two goons in Drago's world before they auctioned me off to Drago himself. He pauses at a door, glancing down the hallway before opening it, and shoves me inside. "This way, Sophia," he urged, his voice steady but tinged with urgency. The stale air of the cellar grew colder as the wall of barrels shifted, revealing a tunnel that exuded an unsettling dampness. My breath caught in my throat, the darkness pressing in, alive and suffocating. The tunnel stretched endlessly into the unknown, its oppressive silence broken only by the faint, rhythmic sound of dripping water. Rossi pulled a flashlight from his pocket, the pale beam cutting through the gloom. "Stay close," he warned, his voice echoing faintly, as if swallowed by the encroaching shadows.

Once we reached the end of the tunnel, it opened into a spacious garage, and inside sat four very expensive cars. The cars gleamed under the faint glow of hidden lights, their sleek designs hinting at untold wealth. Rossi stepped closer, scanning the surroundings cautiously. "These," he said, his voice low, "are our ticket out. But first, we need to make sure no one followed us." He pulled out a small device and scanned the area. After a moment, he nodded. "We're clear," he said. "Let's get moving." He opened the door of the nearest car, and I climbed in, my heart racing as we prepared to make our escape. Rossi then climbed into the driver's seat, taking off like a bat out of hell, making me hold on for dear life. "I am so sorry, Sophia, but it needs to be like this. He can't let you get caught, and Drago himself ordered me to get you out of here quickly. He says he will fly out and visit us as soon as he can," he says, trying to calm me down.

I watched as he passed through all the security gates with ease. He parked the car next to a private plane that looked incredibly expensive. "Wow," I whispered, though the word caught in my throat. The jet was dazzling, but instead of excitement, a deep sense of dread coiled in my chest.

"Yes, it is... this is Nico's private jet," Rossi says as we climb the stairs to board. Walking in, I glance around at the exquisite interior. Wow is an understatement. This plane was amazing. Not that I expected anything less from these men. "Go ahead and sit down and make yourself comfortable. It's going to be a long flight."

19

SAFE HAVEN, OR IS IT?

I glanced out the window at the clouds zooming by and saw nothing but the clouds and the wings of the airplane. I was sitting in my seat. I glanced over at Rossi only to find him asleep in his seat. His head was tilted back against the headrest, and the chair was kicked back. He looked so relaxed, and it made me curse, wishing I could just will myself to sleep. But I can't. I haven't slept in a moving vehicle since my parents' accident, no matter what it was. I envied his ability to sleep so easily. The hum of the engines and the gentle rocking of the plane did nothing to lull me. Instead, my mind raced with thoughts, unable to escape the memories that kept me awake.

I stood up and went to the back of the plane, where his private bedroom was located, as well as the bathroom. After releasing my bladder, I decided to lie down on the bed and see if I could sleep that way. After all, maybe things would be different if I lay down on a bed rather than sitting in a chair. *Who would have thought one's life could change so drastically in just a few short days? I mean, my life is a train wreck now.*

"Hey, we are here." I heard a deep voice say as I struggled to open my eyes and blink up. I found Rossi standing in the doorway, looking at me. I slowly sat up, rubbing my eyes, trying to shake off the grogginess. The reality of my new circumstances hit me again, like a weight I couldn't shake. I followed Rossi out, unsure of what awaited me but knowing I had no choice but to face it. Stepping out of the plane, I saw several black luxury cars waiting. These cars were flanked by several men with massive, well-built bodies dressed in typical black suits and sunglasses, trying to hide the fact that they were there to provide us with security. The men escorted us to one of the cars, their presence both reassuring and intimidating. As we drove through unfamiliar streets, I couldn't help but wonder what awaited me. The weight of my situation pressed down, but I knew I had to stay alert.

"It is a pleasure to have you back, sir, and who is this beautiful lady?" I hear the man ask who sits in the front seat of the car.

"Thanks, Donte, it really is great to be back." I hear Rossi respond, which makes me wonder if he's been here before. "This is my fiancée."

"Wait, what?" I blurt out, only to have Rossi cover my mouth.

"Don't blow our cover. I'll explain more once we get home." He whispered in my ear before removing his hand. I nodded, realizing the importance of staying quiet. The car ride felt endless as tension filled the air. Finally, we arrived at a grand estate, its gates opening silently. Inside, Rossi pulled me aside, his expression serious. "This is bigger than you think," he said, his voice low and urgent. "We're dealing with dangerous people, and they can't know who you really are. Trust me, this is for your safety." His tone left no room for argument. I nodded, swallowing hard, as the reality of our situation sank in.

As we entered the enormous mansion, I marveled at the furnishings and decor. Everything looked pristine and luxurious, from the intricate chandeliers to the polished marble floors. The air smelled faintly of expensive perfume and fresh flowers, adding to the overwhelming sense of opulence. Despite the beauty surrounding me, I couldn't shake off the unease that had settled in my stomach. "My darling, this is my home." Rossi smiles at me as I look around. I couldn't help but feel out of place, as if I didn't belong in this world of wealth and power. Rossi's reassuring smile did little to ease my nerves. The weight of his earlier words lingered, reminding me of the danger we were in.

"Anita," I heard him call out a name before I saw a sweet, young, innocent-looking girl dressed in a typical black and white maid uniform come forward. "Please, take my future wife to her room. She will rest in a guest room until the wedding. She needs to get settled in, while I handle some urgent business matters." Anita nodded and gestured for me to follow her up a grand staircase. I trailed behind, my heart racing as I took in my surroundings. The house felt more like a museum than a home, and I couldn't help but wonder what Rossi's "urgent business matters" entailed. She opens a single wooden door into a stunning bedroom with light blue walls and white trim. I glanced at the king-sized four-poster bed, dressed in white with silver throw pillows. It looked comfortable to me. A white wintery scene was depicted on the wall over the bed, and on each side sat white tables with light blue lamps. The room had a desk and a dresser on each side of the bed, as well as a bathroom with light blue towels and rugs. "Thank you," I say before she leaves. I stepped inside and closed the door, feeling a mix of awe and unease. The room was beautiful but intimidating, much like everything else in this place. I sat on the edge of the bed, wondering what I had gotten myself into.

Not knowing what to do, I decided to change into something more comfortable. I step into the walk-in closet, amazed at all the clothes inside. Finding a pair of drawstring cotton pajama pants, I slide them on and select a matching tank top. After discovering a pair of fuzzy slippers, I put them on and returned to the room. I found Rossi standing in the middle of it. "Rossi," I said, trying to hide my surprise. "What are you doing here?"

He smiled, scanning the room. "I wanted to make sure you were settled in," he replied, his tone casual yet unnerving. I nodded, unsure of what to say next.

"I'm fine, but I don't know what to do or say to play this part," I admit. "I never wanted to be Drago's fiancée in the first place, and now I have to act like I'm yours."

"I understand," Rossi said, his expression softening. "But we have to make this believable. Just follow my lead, and I'll help you through it. Trust me, it'll work out." I nodded, still unsure but willing to try. "Are you hungry?" He asked.

"A little," I admit, my stomach growling softly. "But I'm more nervous than anything."

Rossi nodded, his gaze steady. "Let's grab something to eat, and we can talk more. It'll ease your nerves." I hesitated but followed him, hoping he was right. We walked to the dining room, where a table was set with a variety of dishes. The aroma of food filled the air, making my stomach growl again. Rossi pulled out a chair for me, and I sat down, trying to calm my nerves. The table was filled with delicious dishes, but I felt uneasy.

"Where are we?" I asked him.

"We are in the only place Drago thought they wouldn't look, Italy. Mr. Russo's men will never suspect we'd hide here," Rossi explained, his voice low. "It's the perfect place to lay low and plan our next move." I glanced around, taking in the grandeur of the room, feeling a mix of fear and awe.

"Okay, whose home is this?" I asked.

"This is the home of an old friend of mine," Rossi replied, his tone cautious. "Someone who owes me a favor and won't ask questions. It's safe here, for now." His words did little to ease my anxiety, but I knew I had no choice but to trust him. I took a deep breath and tried to focus on the food in front of me. The flavors were rich and comforting, but my mind was racing with questions. Who was this friend? And how long could we really stay hidden here? I was so scared, scared that Mr. Russo would find me. I knew what he meant to do with me, if he ever found me. He'll kill me, Drago told me he would. I couldn't shake the feeling of dread, no matter how much I tried to distract myself. The thought of Mr. Russo's men finding us here made my heart race. I had to trust Rossi, but the uncertainty of our situation was overwhelming. I forced myself to eat, trying to steady my nerves. The silence in the room was heavy, broken only by the faint sound of distant traffic. I couldn't help but wonder if this sanctuary was truly as secure as Rossi claimed.

20

I WILL FIGHT UNTIL MY LAST BREATH

I slowly opened my eyes, sat up in bed, and released a soft sigh. I didn't know what to expect today, and I was on edge after having nightmares all night long. I jump at the sound of a knock on the bedroom door. "Come in," I respond, and watch as Rossi enters the room fully dressed in a suit and tie.

"I have some bad news. I have to head into the office and do some work. I'm wondering if you'll accompany me there," he asked.

"Sure," I replied, trying to hide my unease. "Let me get ready." As I get dressed, my mind races with possibilities. What could be so urgent? I can't shake the feeling that something is wrong, but I push it aside and get dressed. I was wearing a dark green button-up blouse, black slacks, a black business jacket, and forest green heels on my feet. I finish getting ready and meet Rossi at the front door.

As we walk to his car, I can't help but feel a sense of foreboding. The drive to his office is silent, and I can tell he's preoccupied. When we arrive, he ushers me into his office and closes the door behind us. “Take a seat,” he says, gesturing to a chair. I sit down, my heart racing as I wait for him to speak. He takes a deep breath and looks at me with a serious expression. “There’s been a development,” he begins, “and it’s not good.”

“What?”

“It’s Drago,” he confesses, his voice heavy with the weight of the truth. “He lost the fight to Mr. Russo. He’s getting married to Luciana... today.”

The words hit me like a physical blow, shattering my composure. My heart plummeted, my pulse raced, and my vision blurred as though the very walls of the room were closing in around me.

I feel a wave of shock wash over me. “Married? Today? How is that possible?”

Rossi sighed heavily. “It’s a long story, but the bottom line is that Drago has no choice. The marriage is part of an agreement he made for your safety. The most impressive part about this is that he asked Nico to come and get you. I guess you are now officially engaged to Nico.”

My mind races as I try to process the news. I feel a mix of emotions—anger, confusion, and disbelief. “Engaged to Nico? How could he do this to me?”

Rossi looked at me sympathetically. “I know it’s a lot to take in, but it’s for your safety. Drago had no other choice.”

I look at Rossi, my voice trembling as I speak. “Am I just supposed to accept this?” I snap, my voice cracking. “Marry Nico, just like that?”

He nodded slowly. “It’s the only way to keep you safe,” he says, his tone firm but gentle. “It’s what Drago wants.”

“What Drago wants?” I ask, dizzy.

“Yes,” Rossi replied. “He’s doing this because he cares about you. It’s the only way to ensure your protection.”

I take a deep breath, steadying myself. “But what about what I want?” I ask. My voice barely rises above a whisper.

“I understand your feelings, but this decision wasn’t made lightly,” Rossi said. “It’s about more than just you—it’s about protecting everyone involved. Drago is doing what he believes is best.” I looked away, tears welling up, realizing the weight of the situation.

Hours later...

I was still sitting in the chair when Rossi delivered the horrible news. The door opens, and I glance up with my tear-blurred eyes, recognizing Nico as he enters the office. I wipe my eyes, trying to compose myself as he approaches. His presence feels suffocating, and I can’t help but resent the circumstances forcing us together. “This is what’s best,” Nico says quietly, his voice lacking any warmth. I clench my fists, feeling trapped and powerless. “Drago knows, with me, you’ll be safe and cared for.”

I meet his gaze, my anger simmering beneath the surface. “Safe? Cared for?” I spit out the words, my voice trembling. “Or controlled? You don’t know me. You don’t get to decide my life.” Nico’s expression hardens, but he says nothing, leaving me to stew in my frustration. “You have no right,” I say, my voice low and steady. “You think you can just step in and take control? I won’t let that happen.”

Nico’s jaw tightens, and for a moment, I see a flicker of uncertainty in his eyes. But it’s gone as quickly as it came. “You don’t have a choice,” he says. His tone is cold and final. “Now let’s go. We have a wedding to attend after all. I am the best man.”

“What, you mean you expect me to attend the wedding, taking him away from me?” I snapped out.

"Yes," he said, his voice unyielding. "This is how it has to be." I stared at him, my heart pounding with rage and despair. I couldn't believe this was happening, that my life was being ripped away, and I was powerless to stop it. He grabs my wrist, yanking me to a standing position before dragging me behind him.

I try to pull away, but his grip is firm. "Let go of me!" I yell, my voice echoing through the empty hallway.

Nico doesn't flinch. "You're coming with me, and you'll do as you're told," he says, his voice cold and commanding.

I struggle against his grip, my anger boiling over. "You can't do this!" I scream, but he doesn't waver. His hold tightens as he drags me forward, leaving me helpless and trapped in his control. Upon leaving the building, he shoves me into the back of a limo before climbing in behind me. The limo's door slams shut, sealing me in with him. I glare, my chest heaving with fury, but he remains unmoved. The car starts to move, and I feel a cold realization settle in—I'm trapped, with no escape, as my future slips further away. The limo speeds through the city, each passing moment feeling like an eternity. I press my face against the window, watching the world blur outside, knowing there's no way out. Nico's presence looms beside me, a constant reminder of my helplessness. My future is no longer mine.

I watch as the limo glides into the airport and pulls next to the same plane that brought me here. "Come on, we need to take off soon." I hear Nico demand and grab my wrist again, pulling me out of the limo. I fought him. I didn't want to be taken to Drago's wedding. I struggled against his grip, desperate to resist, but he overpowered me effortlessly. As he drags me toward the plane, my heart races with dread. I know I can't escape, and the thought of facing Drago fills me with deep, unyielding dread. Nico's grip tightens as he forces me up the steps. My resistance fades, replaced by a numb acceptance of what's to come. The plane door closes behind us, sealing my fate. I'm trapped, powerless, as the engines roar to life, carrying me toward a future I dread. "You need to accept this." I sink into the seat, defeated. The plane ascends, and the world below disappears. I close my eyes, trying to block out the reality of my situation. But the weight of my helplessness presses down, suffocating any hope of freedom.

"I don't need to accept anything. Before Drago claimed me as his, I was doing pretty well. This is all his fault!" I screamed out. "I had a life, dreams, and freedom before he took it all away. Now, I'm just a pawn in his game, forced into a future I never wanted. I won't forgive him for this—never." I'll never forget what he's done to me, and I'll never stop fighting for my freedom. Even if it seems impossible now, I'll find a way to escape his grasp and reclaim the life that was stolen from me.

"Are you done?" he asked. "Because I need you to go into the room and put the dress lying on the bed on. When this plane lands, we are heading straight to the wedding venue."

"No, I'm not done. I refuse to put that dress on." I reply, glaring back at him.

"You will put it on," he said firmly, his voice leaving no room for argument. "You belong to me now, and you will do as I say." His words cut through me like a knife, but I refused to give in.

"I don't belong to anyone," I spat back, my voice trembling with defiance. "You can force me into that dress, but you'll never own my spirit. I'll fight you every step of the way, no matter what it takes."

Nico straightened up, stepping closer. His eyes focused on me. "You're right, I can force you into the dress, force you to go with me to the wedding, and watch Drago marry that girl. You're right, but you're wrong about the rest because you will stop fighting about this. Because the minute you arrive at the wedding, they will watch you like a hawk. Any deviation from the plan, Mr. Russo will pull the trigger and kill you. This arranged marriage is the only thing keeping you alive."

I stared at him, my chest heaving with anger and fear. "You think I'll just comply? You're wrong. I'll find a way out, no matter the cost."

Nico grabbed me up from my seat, his eyes cold. "You won't. Because if you try, you'll die, and I won't let that happen." His grip tightened, leaving me breathless and unsure of my next move. I trembled in his grip, my defiance wavering under the weight of his words. The cold certainty in his eyes sent a chill down my spine. For the first time, I wondered if resistance was truly worth the risk—or if survival meant surrendering to their control.

21

IS THIS REAL?

I stood before the full-length mirror, the silk of the wedding dress pressing against my skin like chains. My reflection stared back, unrecognizable in a gown I hadn't chosen. My heart pounded in my chest—this wasn't Drago and Lucianna's day. It was mine, stolen.

"They decided to marry us right afterward, so there isn't any temptation," I heard Nico say from the doorway. "You'll both be married off."

The words hung in the air, heavy and final. I felt trapped, suffocated by the weight of a decision I hadn't made.

I felt a mix of shock and confusion wash over me. This was supposed to be their day, not mine. Yet, here I was, about to be married without any warning or preparation. My mind raced as I tried to process what was happening. "Remember, I promised Drago I'd protect you. That is all I am trying to do here. To keep you safe." I couldn't believe what I was hearing. Protect me? This wasn't protection; it felt like a betrayal. I wanted to protest, to scream, but the words caught in my throat. My heart pounded as I stared at my reflection, realizing my life was about to change forever.

"I can't do this," I whispered, my throat tightening as though the cabin air had thinned. The pilot's announcement of our descent brought the full weight of the situation crashing down on me. The reality of what lay ahead hit me like a tidal wave, leaving me breathless and overwhelmed. My hands tremble, and my throat tightens. I can't go through with this, but I know I have no choice. I take a deep breath, trying to steady myself as the plane touches down. The weight of what's about to happen presses on me, and I feel trapped. This wasn't how my life was supposed to unfold, yet here I am, powerless to stop it.

"Come now, Sophia. They are waiting for us." Nico says, holding out his hand. I reluctantly place my hand in his, feeling the warmth of his grip. As we step off the plane, warm air surrounds me, and I know there's no turning back. My fate is sealed, and I must face whatever lies ahead, whether I'm ready or not. He leads me to a dark green car, opens the back door, and helps me inside before jumping behind the wheel. I gaze out the window, watching the landscape blur past, feeling a mix of dread and uncertainty. The car's engine hums steadily, matching my racing thoughts. This is my new reality, and I can only hope I find the strength to endure it. We pull up to the hotel. My heart races as I get out of the car. Standing at the top of the steps is none other than Drago Morelli himself. To his right stood Mr. Russo. His face was grim as he watched Nico and I stand hand in hand. Nico leads me toward them, and my legs feel like lead. I force myself to keep walking, my heart pounding in my chest. As we approach, Drago's eyes lock on mine, and I can't help but feel a chill run down my spine.

"I am glad you could make it, Sophia. I hope Nico filled you in on the changes." Drago says in a smooth, calm voice.

"Yes, he did," I replied, trying to steady my voice. Drago nodded, his gaze never leaving mine.

"Good," he says. "Then you understand the importance of what's about to happen." I swallow hard, feeling the weight of his words. "You do, don't you?" he pressed, his tone sharp. I nodded, though uncertainty still gnawed at me. Drago's smirk sent a wave of unease through me. "Perfect," he said, turning to Mr. Russo. "Let's begin."

We followed them into the hotel, through the busy lobby. I caught sight of Jenny and smiled at her as I walked by, wishing I could have told her what was happening. The lobby's commotion faded as Drago led us to a private meeting room. My mind raced with questions, but I dared not speak. The air grew heavy with tension, and I gripped Nico's hand tightly, bracing myself for whatever was about to unfold. Once inside, I saw the pastor standing beneath a beautiful rose arch. In front of him stood Luciana. She, too, wore a beautiful wedding gown. She looked at me, and Nico pulled me forward. He stood next to me, while Drago stood next to Luciana. "Let's get this over with," Drago growled out. It was then that I knew he was unhappy about the way things had unfolded. He shot a glare at Luciana, who avoided his gaze, her hands trembling slightly. The pastor cleared his throat, his voice steady as he began the ceremony. Nico's grip on my hand tightened, his breath shallow. I could feel the weight of the moment pressing down on us all, the air thick with unspoken fears and regrets.

"Do you, Drago Morelli, take Mrs. Sophia Quinn to be your lawfully wedded wife? To have and hold, for rich or poorer, in sickness and in health, for as long as you both shall live?" he asked out loud.

"Wait a minute. What do you think you are doing? It's Luciana Russo whom he's marrying, not Sophia. Get it straight." Demanded Mr. Russo in anger. The pastor hesitated, glancing between the couples in confusion. Nico's grip on my hand loosened as he exchanged a tense look with Drago. Luciana's trembling grew more pronounced, her eyes darting nervously. The air was thick with tension, and I could sense the fragile balance of the situation teetering on the edge of chaos.

"My apologies, I was told that Drago was with Sophia, and Luciana was with Nico." The pastor exclaimed in a fright at Mr. Russo. The pastor's voice wavered as he corrected himself, "Do you, Drago Morelli, take Luciana Russo to be your lawfully wedded wife?" Drago's hesitation lingered, his gaze locked with Nico's. Luciana's breath hitched, her hand trembling visibly as the room fell into an uneasy silence.

"I do," he finally said, his eyes locking onto mine. The weight of his words hung heavy in the air, a mix of resolve and regret. Luciana's grip tightened on her bouquet, her eyes glistening with unshed tears. Nico's jaw clenched, his silence speaking volumes. The pastor, visibly relieved, continued the ceremony, but the atmosphere remained charged with unspoken tension.

"Do you, Luciana Russo, take Drago Morelli to be your lawfully wedded husband?" the pastor asked. Luciana's voice wavered as she replied, "I do," her words barely audible. The pastor rushed through the vows, but the tension in the room remained palpable. As the couple exchanged rings, their forced smiles did little to mask the turmoil beneath the surface. Then the pastor faced Nico and I and began our vows. "Do you, Nico Moretti, take Sophia Quinn to be your lawfully wedded wife?"

"I do," Nico said firmly, his voice steady despite the storm brewing in his eyes.

"Do you, Sophia Quinn, take Nico Moretti as your lawfully wedded husband?" the pastor asked me, and my heart sank. I didn't want to answer, knowing what was expected of me. "I do," I whispered, my voice trembling. The weight of my words hung heavy in the air, mingling with the unspoken emotions that filled the room. The pastor nodded, his expression solemn, as he declared us husband and wife.

"Good, now that you are both married, Sophia is safe from me and my men." Mr. Russo declares before leaving the room.

Drago rushed up to me, "I'm so sorry, Sophia, I didn't want to do this to you," he explained. Drago's apology hung in the air, heavy with regret. His eyes, filled with a mix of guilt and helplessness, met mine for a fleeting moment before he turned away, unable to bear the weight of what he had done. The silence that followed was suffocating, broken only by the sound of Nico's steady breathing beside me.

"I told you, this wasn't what he wanted," Nico said, his voice heavy with regret. My chest tightened as Drago and Lucianna walked away, the weight of betrayal settling deep within me. I knew Nico's words were true—Drago's forced sacrifice had saved me from something far worse, but the cost was a burden we both carried. The realization hit me like a wave: this union, born out of necessity, would bind us in ways neither of us had ever wanted. "Come on, I need to show you our new rooms," Nico said, gently taking my hand and pulling me out of the room toward the elevator.

"Wait, new rooms?" I asked.

"Yep, you and I have been moved to a smaller suite on the floor under the penthouse," he admitted as he pushed the button to call the elevator.

"Why?" I asked, my voice barely above a whisper.

"It's part of the deal, you and I have to live separately from Drago and Luciana," he admitted. I nodded slowly, trying to process his words. The elevator door opened, and we stepped inside. The silence between us was heavy with unspoken emotions. We rode the elevator in silence, both caught up in our own thoughts. Once the elevator stopped and opened, he led me down the hallway, pausing at one of the few doors on this floor. He takes out his room key, slides it into the slot, and the door unlocks. We both stepped inside. The suite was much smaller than our penthouse, but it felt cozy. The space was modest but well-furnished, with a small living area and two bedrooms. Nico turned to me, his expression unreadable. "I know it's not what we're used to, but it's only temporary," he said, trying to sound reassuring. I nodded, unsure of what to say.

"So, where's my room?" I asked him.

"It's the one on the left," he replied, pointing to the door. I nodded and entered, taking in the elegant furnishings. "We will be sharing this room, as you are my wife," Nico said as he stood just inside the door, watching me glance around the room. I felt a mix of surprise and unease at his words. The room was beautiful, but the thought of sharing it with him brought a wave of tension. I turned to face him, trying to mask my uncertainty, as he continued to watch me closely. "I'll give you some time to settle in," he said, before stepping out and closing the door behind him. I took a deep breath, trying to calm my nerves.

22

PLOT TWIST

Opening my eyes, I almost jumped out of bed at the shock of seeing Nico sleeping soundly beside me. I had to remind myself that I was now married to this man. I would have to get used to waking up like this. I slid out of bed and went to the bathroom. I stared at my reflection, thinking about the previous night's events. About Drago's confession, and what it really meant to him to save my life. In so doing, he trapped me into this marriage, and I couldn't have been madder that I was forced into this life. I decided I needed a long soak in the tub and filled the tub with water. I let the warm water fill the tub, hoping it would help me relax and clear my mind. As I sank into the soothing water, I couldn't help but feel trapped in this new reality. My thoughts kept drifting back to Drago's confession, and the weight of it all felt unbearable.

The door creaked open, and Nico stepped inside. Startled, I instinctively stood up, clutching a towel to shield myself, my heart racing. "What are you doing?!" I exclaimed, my voice trembling as water splashed over the edge of the tub.

Nico looked at me with a mixture of confusion and concern. "I just wanted to check on you," he said softly. "You've been in here a while." His voice was calm, but I couldn't shake the feeling of unease. I wrapped the towel tighter around myself, my heart racing.

I stared at him, unsure of what to say. "I'm fine," I muttered, though my trembling voice betrayed me.

Nico hesitated before nodding and stepping back. "Alright," he said, closing the door behind him. I sank back into the water, feeling more trapped than ever. I quickly washed my body and hair before climbing out of the tub and getting dressed.

Stepping out of the room, into our shared living space, I saw Nico sitting at the table with his laptop in front of him. I sat down across from him, trying to steady my nerves. "We need to talk about what happened," I said, my voice trembling.

Nico looked up, his expression unreadable. "I know," he replied, closing his laptop. "And we will. Just not right now."

I nodded slowly, my mind racing with questions. "When?" I asked, my voice barely above a whisper.

He looked at me, his eyes softening. "Soon," he said, his tone firm but gentle. "I promise." I took a deep breath, trying to steady myself.

I stood back up, heading to the kitchen. Fine, if he chose to ignore me, then I would get busy. "Are you hungry?" I asked him. "I'll make something," I said, opening the fridge. I needed a distraction, something to keep my hands busy and my mind off the tension between us. Cooking had always been my way of coping, and right now, I needed it more than ever. I started pulling out ingredients, the familiar motions calming me slightly. Nico remained silent, watching me. I could feel his eyes on my back as I chopped vegetables, the rhythmic motion grounding me. I grab a frying pan and crack a few eggs into a bowl. Omelets sound really delicious to me. I whisked the eggs and added a pinch of salt and pepper. As the pan heated, I glanced over my shoulder. Nico still hadn't moved, his gaze fixed on me. I focused on the sizzle of the butter in the pan, hoping the meal might ease the tension between us. As I plated the omelets, I turned to see Nico still watching me. "Let's eat," I said, setting the table. The silence lingered, but the familiar act of sharing a meal felt like a small step toward bridging the gap between us.

Nico picked up his fork, his movements slow and deliberate. I waited, unsure if he would speak or if the silence would last indefinitely. Finally, he took a bite, and I exhaled, hoping that this small gesture might mend what felt broken. "This is good. Where did you learn to cook?" he asked, a hint of curiosity in his voice.

I smiled, relieved by the question, and replied, "From my grandmother. She taught me everything I know about cooking."

He nodded, taking another bite. "She must have been a remarkable woman." I felt warmth spread through me.

"She was," I said softly. "And I think she'd be happy to know that her lessons still bring people together."

Nico's expression softened as he listened, a gentle smile tugging at the corners of his lips. "It's amazing how food can connect generations," he mused, his eyes reflecting a newfound appreciation. "I'm glad you shared that with me."

"You are welcome, so tell me. What am I supposed to do now?" I asked, feeling unsure about my life. What did he expect from me, now that I was his wife? He hesitated, his gaze thoughtful.

"For now, just be yourself," he said, his tone gentle yet firm. "Take your time to settle in, and we'll figure things out together. There's no rush." His words, though simple, carried a weight of reassurance, and I felt a flicker of hope stir within me.

"I have no clue what you mean. Just be myself. What is my day going to be like? What do you expect of me? Am I going to be forced to bear your children? “I don’t know about that,” he replied, his voice steady. “What I do know is that I want you to feel comfortable and supported. Let’s take things one step at a time, and we’ll build this life together, however it unfolds.” I felt a mix of relief and confusion swirling inside me. The uncertainty of our future loomed large, yet his words offered a comforting promise that I wasn’t alone in navigating this new chapter. It was daunting, but the thought of building something together, step by step, filled me with a cautious optimism that maybe, just maybe, everything would turn out all right.

His phone rang, and I watched as he pulled it out of his pocket. “Shit, what now?” he asks before answering. “Yeah, boss. What’s up?” He listened intently for a moment, his expression shifting to one of mild annoyance. “Alright, I’ll handle it,” he said, ending the call. Turning back to me, he offered a faint smile. “Looks like duty calls. Let’s talk more later, okay?” He leaned in, kissed my forehead, and headed for the door. As I watched him leave, I couldn’t help but wonder what challenges lay ahead. “Stay here, I’ll send Rossi to watch you and keep you safe.” I nodded, trying to mask my unease. As the door closed behind him, the weight of the unknown pressed down on me. I couldn’t shake the feeling that our fragile sense of normalcy was slipping away, replaced by something far more unpredictable and dangerous.

An hour later...

Hearing a knock on the door, I head over to it. “Whose there?” I yell out. “It’s me, Rossi,” a gruff voice replies. I hesitated, my hand on the doorknob, my mind racing with doubt. The voice didn’t sound like his. I cautiously opened the door, only to have it shoved open, and I was knocked down to the floor. I glanced up at Mr. Russo. He loomed over me, his expression unreadable. “You’re coming with me,” he growls, grabbing my arm roughly. Panic surged as I tried to resist, but his grip was unyielding. He dragged me through the door, my feet stumbling as I fought to break free.

Fear was suffocating, but I refused to give in. "Let go of me!" I screamed. My voice cracked. He didn't respond, his silence terrifying. I clawed at his hand, my nails scraping against his skin, but he didn't flinch. The cold determination in his eyes sent a chill down my spine. He dragged me further into the unknown, and I knew then that escape was slipping further from my grasp. "Why are you doing this? Drago married Luciana, you forced me to marry Nico!" I screamed at him. He remained silent, his grip tightening as he pulled me down the dimly lit hallway. My heart raced, my mind reeling with unanswered questions. The air grew heavier with tension, and I realized this was no mere misunderstanding—it was a deliberate act, and I was at his mercy. The hallway seemed endless, each step taking me deeper into a nightmare. His silence only amplified my dread, as if words would somehow lessen the terror. I struggled to think, to plan, but his grip was a constant reminder of my helplessness. The dim lights flickered, casting eerie shadows that seemed to mock my plight.

As we approached the elevator, I watched in horror as the door opened to reveal Drago and Luciana inside. Their faces were expressionless, their eyes cold and unyielding. I felt a wave of despair wash over me, realizing they were all in this together. The elevator door closed, sealing my fate. I was trapped, surrounded by enemies, with no way out. "Dad, what are you doing?" Luciana asked. I glanced in her direction, only to see Drago silencing her. The elevator descended in silence, the air thick with unspoken menace. I could feel Luciana's eyes on me, pleading and fearful, but Drago's presence stifled any defiance. The flickering lights mirrored my growing dread as I braced myself for whatever awaited us at our destination.

Mr. Russo's voice cut through the air like a whip. "Put her in the limo," he barked, his tone leaving no room for argument. Drago's grip tightened on my arm, his fingers digging into my skin as I stumbled, my feet scraping against the rough pavement. Luciana's eyes, wide with terror, met mine for a fleeting moment, her silent plea echoing the fear that gripped my own heart.

The ride was silent, but the tension in the air was suffocating. Luciana's gaze flickered between me and her father, her fear a living thing, impossible to ignore. I knew, with a sinking certainty, that whatever lay ahead would be far worse than anything I had endured so far. The city lights blurred past the windows, their glow a cruel mockery of my helplessness.

Finally, the car slowed to a stop in front of a dimly lit warehouse. The massive steel doors stood like a barrier to the unknown, their cold, unyielding presence sending a chill down my spine.

Mr. Russo stepped out first, his expression grim. Drago shoved me forward, and I stumbled into the cold, echoing space. Luciana hesitated, her trembling hand reaching for mine, but Drago yanked her away. "Stop, you know we have to do this," He said.

23

THE NONSENSE HAS ESCALATED

She pulled back, her eyes wide with fear. "Please," she whispered, her voice barely audible. Drago's grip tightened, his face set in a determined scowl. I glanced at Mr. Russo, hoping for a sign of mercy, but his gaze was fixed straight ahead, unyielding. He stopped in front of a heavy steel door and nodded at Drago, who shoved me inside. "I'm sorry, Sophia... I can't get over you. He's forcing me to do this." The door slammed shut, and darkness enveloped me like a living presence. My breath caught, and I felt trapped, utterly alone. The room was cold and damp, the silence suffocating. My heart pounded as I fumbled in the darkness, searching desperately for something, anything, to ground myself. The sound of the door locking echoed in my mind, a cruel reminder of my isolation. I was trapped, alone, and terrified. Panic clawed at my throat, and I struggled to steady my breathing. Questions raced through my mind: How long would I be here? Would anyone come to my rescue? The darkness seemed to close in on me, amplifying my fears and the chilling uncertainty of my fate. In the silence, I tried to cling to the hope that Luciana's hesitation meant she might still help me, that somehow, I wasn't entirely alone in this nightmare.

Days go by with nothing. No one comes to my rescue, and no water or food is given to me. I'm lying on the cold ground, waiting for death to take me. My body grows weaker, my thoughts foggy. I try to hold on to hope, but it slips away with each passing hour. The silence is broken only by my faint whispers of desperation. I wonder if anyone will ever find me, or if this is how my story ends. Suddenly, the silence is shattered as the door bursts open, and Nico stands there, gun in hand, his eyes scanning the room until they lock onto mine. Relief floods through me as he rushes forward, his voice a mixture of urgency and reassurance. "I've got you," he says, pulling me into his arms. "You're safe now," he whispers, his grip tightening. My body trembles, but his presence anchors me. As he helps me to my feet, I realize that hope, fragile as it was, had never truly left me.

He guided me out of the warehouse, helping me into his car's front seat. He jumps behind the wheel and drives. "I'm going to kill him, force me to marry a woman, and then steal her and lock her up without food and water. What the hell was he thinking?" Nico growled out through his clenched teeth. "He's going to regret ever crossing me. No one messes with what's mine and gets away with it." His grip on the steering wheel tightened, his knuckles turning white. I could feel the anger radiating off him, but beneath it, there was a fierce determination to protect me at all costs. His voice was low and steady, filled with a quiet resolve that left no room for doubt. "I won't let anyone hurt you again," he said, his eyes fixed on the road ahead. The night air was cool and crisp as we sped down the deserted highway, the full moon casting a silvery glow over the landscape. Tall trees lined the road, their shadows stretching across the asphalt like dark sentinels watching our escape. The occasional flicker of headlights in the distance was the only sign of life, as if the world had paused, holding its breath in anticipation of what was to come.

It wasn't until he turned the car onto a small winding road, pulling to a stop in front of a huge iron gate, did I dared ask him anything. "Where are we?" I asked him in a hoarse voice.

He hesitated for a moment, his grip tightening on the steering wheel, before answering. "Somewhere safe," he said, his voice barely above a whisper. The gate creaked open slowly, revealing a hidden path leading to a secluded house nestled among the trees. "This is my mother's house, or it was my mother's house. She passed away over ten years ago, and I haven't come here since. Drago doesn't know anything about this place. I hope you'll be safe here," he explains. The house stood silent and still, as if time had stopped within its walls. He led me inside, the air thick with memories and the faint scent of lavender. "You should be safe here," he repeated, his voice trembling slightly. "But you must promise me one thing -- don't leave, no matter what."

"I don't understand," I said, my voice trembling as much as his. "What's going on? Why are we here?"

He looked at me, his eyes filled with fear and determination. "I can't explain everything right now," he said. "Just trust me, please. It's for your safety. I know you have questions," he continued, his voice steadying. "But for now, you need to stay hidden. There are people looking for you, and this is the only place I can think of where they won't find you."

"Who's looking for me? Apart from Mr. Russo and Drago?" I asked him as he handed me a bottle of water.

"It's better if you don't know all the details right now," he said, avoiding my gaze. "Just stay quiet, keep the doors locked, and don't let anyone in. I'll be back as soon as I can." With that, he turned and left, leaving me alone with my racing thoughts. I sat there, trying to make sense of his words, but my mind was spinning. Who could be after me? And why? I took a sip of water, trying to calm my nerves, but the fear and uncertainty only grew with each passing moment.

The house was surrounded by dense woods, their towering trees casting long shadows across the yard as the sun dipped below the horizon. An old wooden porch wrapped around the front, creaking softly underfoot with every step. Inside, the rooms were filled with antique furniture, dust-covered picture frames, and faded floral wallpaper that added to the sense of eerie tranquility. I sat on the sofa, nodding off as I finally felt safe enough to sleep. I drifted into a restless sleep, and in my dream, I found myself wandering through an endless forest. The trees loomed ominously, their branches twisting like skeletal fingers reaching out to snatch me. A shadowy figure followed me, always just out of sight, whispering my name with a voice that echoed through the darkness. I ran, my heart pounding, but no matter how fast I moved, the figure seemed to close in, its presence growing more oppressive with every step. Suddenly, I tripped and fell, the ground beneath me vanishing into an abyss. I jolted awake, my heart racing, as the creaking of the porch outside echoed through the silent house. The line between dream and reality blurred, leaving me trembling in the dark.

I slowly stood up, walking through the home. Not wanting to sleep, I got to work on cleaning the house instead. I swept the floors, dusted the furniture, and wiped down the windows, trying to distract myself from the lingering unease. As I worked, the house seemed to creak and groan around me, as if it too were unsettled by the events of the night. When the door burst open, I screamed as a man stormed inside, a gun held in front of him. It was pointed at me, and I raised both my hands. "Who are you, and what do you want? I don't want trouble," I stammered, my voice trembling.

The man's cold gaze bore into me as he stepped closer, the gun unwavering. "Just stay calm," he growled. My throat tightened, sweat dampening my palms as the cold steel of the gun glinted in my vision, sending a shiver of fear through me.

"I don't have much, but you can take whatever you want," I said, trying to sound calm. The man's grip on the gun tightened, and he motioned for me to move toward the living room. My heart pounded as I complied, desperately hoping for a chance to escape.

"Sit down," he demanded, and I sat on the sofa. "Now, listen carefully," he said, his voice cold and steady. "I need you to stay quiet and do exactly as I say." My hands trembled as I nodded, my eyes fixed on the gun. The tension in the room was suffocating, and I could feel my pulse racing. "If you scream or try to run, I won't hesitate to use this," he warned, gesturing toward the gun. I nodded again, my throat tight with fear. The man's eyes never left mine as he took a step back, keeping the weapon trained on me. "Now tell me, where is Nico?"

"I-I don't know," I stammered, my voice trembling.

He cocked the gun, the click echoing in the silence. "Wrong answer," he sneered, his icy gaze sending shivers down my spine. I swallowed hard, desperately trying to think of a way out. The room felt like it was closing in around me. I racked my brain for something, anything, that could help me escape this nightmare. "I swear, I don't know where he is," I pleaded, my voice barely above a whisper. The man's finger hovered over the trigger, and I braced myself for the worst.

"I'm here, you will drop that gun," Nico said, stepping into the room behind me, coming from the kitchen. The man's grip on the gun faltered as he turned toward Nico, his surprise evident. Nico's steely gaze met his unwavering gaze. "Drop it," he repeated, and his voice was firm. I turned and glanced at Nico, who was standing behind me with a gun of his own, pointing at the man.

The man hesitated, his eyes darting between Nico and me. "You don't want to do this," he said, his voice wavering slightly.

Nico's expression remained cold and determined. "I won't ask again," he said, his fingers tightening on the trigger. The man's hand trembled, his grip loosening on the weapon. With a final glance at Nico, he slowly lowered the gun to the floor. Nico kept his aim steady until the man stepped back, hands raised in surrender. "Good choice, now tell me why you are here," Nico demanded.

24

DROP DEAD

The man swallowed hard, his eyes filled with fear and resignation. "Look, I had no choice," he stammered, glancing nervously at the door. "They sent me to kidnap her, but first I had to deliver this, " he explained, holding out an envelope in his hand.

Nico raised an eyebrow. "Who sent you?" Nico asked through his gritted teeth, his weapon still in his hand as he took the envelope from the man. Nico tore open the envelope, scanning the contents with confusion and anger. "This doesn't make sense," he muttered, his grip tightening on the paper.

"Please, if I don't return to him with the girl, he will kill her." I heard the man stutter. Nico's eyes narrowed as he processed the man's words. "Who is he? Kill who?" he demanded, his voice low and dangerous.

The man hesitated, fear etched on his face. "I can't... I can't tell you that," he whispered, his voice trembling. Nico's grip on the weapon tightened, his patience wearing thin.

“See, you’re already too deep in this, as that is my wife you were trying to kidnap,” Nico growled at him. “Tell me who he is, or you will face the consequences.”

The man’s eyes widened in terror as he realized the gravity of the situation. “I-I can’t... please,” he stammered, backing away.

Nico’s expression hardened, his voice cold and unyielding. “You have until three. One... two...” He said, “Three.” His voice was steady, his resolve unwavering. The man’s trembling intensified, but he remained silent, his lips sealed. Nico’s eyes flashed with fury and determination. “You leave me with no choice,” he said, his tone leaving no doubt. A gunshot echoed through the room. The silence that followed was deafening, each second stretching into eternity. Nico lowered the weapon slowly, his gaze fixed on the man’s fallen form.

I froze, my scream catching in my throat as I stared at the lifeless body on the floor. “Sophia, sweetheart. Look at me! It’s Nico. You are safe!” His voice was gentle, but the sight of the blood-soaked body behind him made my stomach clench with horror. I couldn’t stop trembling as I met his eyes, tears streaming down my face. I wanted to believe him, to feel safe, but the sheer terror of what I had just seen was too much to bear. Nico’s voice softened as he stepped closer, his hand gently lifting my chin. “Sophia, I did what I had to,” he said, his eyes searching mine. “I won’t let anyone hurt you.” My heart pounded, and I wanted to scream, to run, but my legs wouldn’t move, my voice trapped in my throat. I wanted to believe he had done it for me, but the image of the lifeless body haunted me, and I couldn’t shake the fear that had taken hold. Nico’s grip on my chin tightened, his eyes pleading for understanding. “You’re safe now, Sophia,” he whispered.

I pulled away from him and wanted to leave the room. I wanted to be away from the lifeless body of the man he had just killed. I stumbled backwards, my heart pounding in my chest. The room felt suffocating, the air thick with what had just happened. I turned and, without thinking, started running. I ran until my legs gave out, collapsing on the cold, hard ground. My chest heaved as I gasped for air. The weight of what had happened pressed down on me. I couldn't escape the image of the lifeless body, the blood, the finality of it all. "I can't do this, I won't do this," I screamed at the large, looming tree in front of me. I curled up, trembling, as the reality of the situation sank in. The world around me felt cold, distant, and unforgiving. I couldn't process the events that had unfolded, and I didn't know how to move forward. All I knew was that I needed to get away, far away, from the horror that had consumed me.

"Sophia, it's okay," I heard him whisper as he scooped me up in his arms. "You'll be alright." I wanted to scream, to push him away, but I couldn't. My body was frozen, my mind numb. His words felt hollow, meaningless against the chaos inside me. I closed my eyes, wishing it all away, but the memory clung to me, unyielding and sharp. I could feel him walking, but I refused to open my eyes. I didn't know where he was taking me, and I didn't care. All I wanted was to forget, to escape the nightmare that had become my reality. But no matter how far we went, the horror followed, etched into my soul, impossible to outrun. Slowly, I felt myself drifting away, slipping into the depths of my subconscious where the pain couldn't reach me. In that space, I floated weightlessly, detached from the world and its harsh truths, seeking solace in the shadows of forgotten dreams.

Opening my eyes, I blinked back at the tears that welled up there. The world around me came into focus, blurry and distorted. Glancing around, I realized I was lying on his bed on his private plane. The soft hum of the plane's engines filled my ears, a strange comfort in the unfamiliar silence. My heart pounded as I sat up. The sheets tangled around me like a reminder of the chaos I longed to leave behind. Standing on my trembling legs, I move to the doorway, glancing out to find Nico sitting in a chair, laptop in his lap, hard at work. I take a deep breath, steadying myself as I try to process the whirlwind of emotions swirling inside me. The weight of the past still clings to me, but I force myself to focus on the present, on the man before me. Nico looks up, his gaze meeting mine, and for a moment, everything else fades away.

"Aw, I see you're awake," he whispers softly. "I'm glad. Are you hungry?" I nod, unsure of what to say. He gestures to the seat across from him, and I sink into it, my body still aching. "I'll get you something," he says, standing up. I watch him walk away, my mind racing with questions I'm not ready to ask. He returns shortly with a tray of food, setting it down before me. "Eat," he says gently. "You need your strength." I pick at the food, my appetite dulled by the storm of thoughts in my head. But his presence is oddly grounding, a tether to something steady in the chaos.

"Where are we going?" I asked softly, almost whispering the question.

He looks at me, his expression unreadable. "Somewhere safe," he says finally, his voice low. "A place where we can figure things out." I nod, though the uncertainty gnaws at me. Safe. The word feels foreign, almost impossible, but I cling to it, hoping it might be true. I force myself to eat some of the food he brought before looking at his computer screen. On it were some property listings.

"Are you buying a house?" I asked him.

He hesitated for a moment, then nodded. "Yes, but not just any house." His voice was steady, yet there was a hint of something more. "It's a place where we can start over, away from all of this. A fresh beginning, for both of us."

"What do you mean, Nico?" I asked him.

He looked at me, his eyes filled with a mix of determination and something I couldn't quite place. "A place where we can be free," he said, his voice barely above a whisper. "Free from the past, from everything that's been holding us back." I felt a flicker of hope, fragile yet persistent, as I considered the possibility of a new beginning. "A place where we can start fresh, and build the life you deserve. Because, Sophia, you deserve everything."

I wanted to believe him, to trust that this could be real. But the doubt lingered, gnawing at me. Could we truly escape the past? Or would it follow us, no matter where we went?

"I want to apologize for what happened in that house. I should have waited for you to leave the room before pulling the trigger and ending that man's life. I should never have let you see it. I am so sorry. I know I can't undo it, but I promise to make it right. To protect you, to give you the life you deserve—a life free from fear and shadows. Together, we can leave it all behind and start fresh."

His voice wavered, but all I could see was the flash of the gun. My stomach knotted as love and fear tore me apart. I wanted to believe Nico, trust his words, and let go of the fear that clung to me like a shadow. Yet, part of me was still haunted by what I'd seen. The memory of that event was etched into my mind. Could I truly trust him again, after everything? I wanted to, with all my heart, but the weight of what I'd witnessed made it so hard to let go.

My heart longed for safety and a fresh start, but my mind kept replaying the moment that shattered my sense of security. I understood his regret and his desire to make amends, but the weight of what I had witnessed was overwhelming. I needed time to process, to find a way to reconcile my emotions with the hope he was offering.

25

SOPHIA, I LOVE YOU

When the plane landed, I followed Nico off the plane. As travelers hurried to their gates, announcements of departures and arrivals reverberated throughout the busy airport. Brightly lit signs pointed towards baggage claims and exits, while freshly brewed coffee smelled from a nearby cafe. I inhaled deeply, savoring the familiar airport aroma. Nico led the way, weaving through the bustling crowd with a practiced ease. I followed him closely, not wanting to lose him in the crowd. “Come, Sophia, this is us.” He said, as I spotted a man holding a sign with MORETTI printed crossed it. Nico grabbed my hand and led me towards the man, his grip firm on my arm.

“Mr. Moretti?” the man greeted, his voice low and professional.

Nico nodded in acknowledgment. “Yes, that’s us,” he confirmed. The man gestured towards a sleek black car parked nearby. Nico guided me to the car, his hand still firmly on my arm, and we settled into the backseat. The driver pulled away smoothly, and I couldn’t help but wonder what awaited us next.

Skyscrapers towered above us, their glass facades reflecting the setting sun's fading light. The streets bustled with life. Cars honked and pedestrians weaved between traffic like a well-practiced dance. Neon signs flickered to life, casting colorful hues onto bustling sidewalks as we sped past. The city is a vibrant tapestry of energy and motion. "Oh my god, are we in New York?" I whispered, my voice trembling with a mix of awe and unease. The towering skyline, dazzling with light, felt less like a symbol of freedom and more like an imposing, unyielding cage of glass.

Nico turned to me, a faint smile playing on his lips. "Yes, we are," he replied, his voice steady. "Welcome to the city that never sleeps." The car continued its smooth journey through the bustling streets, and I couldn't help but feel a mix of excitement and curiosity about what lay ahead. The car slowed to a stop in front of a towering building, its darkened windows reflecting city lights. Nico stepped out, deliberate, and extended a hand to help me out. The air felt heavy, charged with unspoken tension as I followed him inside, unsure of what awaited us. The lobby was dimly lit, its polished floors reflecting the glow of the city outside. Nico's grip on my arm tightened as we stepped into the elevator, and the doors closed with a soft thud.

The elevator ascended swiftly, its silence amplifying the tension. Nico's expression was unreadable, his hand still firm on my arm. I swallowed hard, my heart racing as the numbers on the display climbed higher. The doors finally slid open, revealing a dimly lit hallway. Nico stepped out, pulling me along, and I couldn't shake the feeling that I was walking into something far more dangerous than I had anticipated. Once he reached a pair of doors with the number 689 on them, I watched him pull out a key from his pocket. He opened the door, revealing a spacious, luxurious apartment. Nico ushered me inside, his hand still firm on my arm. The apartment was eerily quiet, its opulence doing little to ease my unease. "Sit," he said, gesturing to a sleek leather couch. I hesitated, my instincts screaming danger, but I complied, my mind racing with possibilities.

He disappeared into another room, and I glanced around at the amazing apartment. Everything seemed pristine, from the polished floors to the modern art on the walls. Yet, the silence felt oppressive, as if the space itself was holding its breath. As he stepped back into the room, "Come, I will show you our room. You can make yourself at home, Sophia, as you are home," he smiled as he led me down a hallway to the master bedroom. The master bedroom was just as lavish as the rest of the apartment, with a king-sized bed and floor-to-ceiling windows offering a breathtaking view of the city. Despite its beauty, I couldn't shake the feeling of unease. Something about this place felt off, and I couldn't quite put my finger on it. I turned to thank him, but he left, disappearing again from view. I turned to the bed and sat at the end of it. My heart pounded as I surveyed the room, searching for any clue about what was happening. The silence grew heavier, and I felt a chill run down my spine. I couldn't shake the feeling that I was being watched, even though I was alone.

"Sophia, we need to talk. I need you to understand that I didn't have a choice about what happened earlier. I had to kill that man to avoid him letting any of my enemies know about you. I have to protect you," he explains, clearing his throat. "Sophia, I love you. You have become my life. I can't let anyone take you from me." He continues, his voice trembling slightly. "I know you're scared, and I don't blame you. But I need you to trust in me. I'll do whatever it takes to keep you safe, no matter the cost." His eyes pleaded with me for understanding.

I nodded slowly, trying to process his words. Despite the fear gripping me, I saw the sincerity in his eyes. "I trust you," I whispered, my voice barely audible. He exhaled, relief washing over his face, and pulled me into a tight embrace.

"Listen up, Sophia. I know this isn't over. But I will do everything in my power to keep you safe and avoid unnecessary mix-ups," he warned. "But if anyone tries to hurt you, I won't hesitate to do what's necessary. You mean too much to me." His grip tightened around me, his determination evident. I nodded, feeling both reassured and uneasy about the path ahead. He held me close, his breath warm against my hair. “We’ll get through this together,” he murmured. “I promise you, Sophia, no matter what happens, I’ll always be here for you.” I closed my eyes, letting his words anchor me in the chaos. His lips brushed mine softly, sending shivers down my spine. I melted into the kiss, momentarily forgetting our troubles. When we pulled apart, his gaze held mine, unwavering. “No matter what,” he repeated, his voice firm. I nodded, clinging to his promise as the world around us seemed to crumble.

He trailed his mouth down my neck, nibbling at my collarbone, causing me to moan. I clung to him, losing myself in the moment, as his lips traced a path back to mine. I surrendered to the moment, my heart racing as his touch ignited fire within me. In his arms, I felt safe, cherished, and alive. The world outside didn’t matter anymore; all that existed was the love we shared, a bond that grew stronger with every passing second. “Shall we move into the bedroom?” He whispered, pulling on my dress. I nodded. My breath caught as he led me towards the bedroom. Anticipation built with every step. Our connection deepened with every touch. As the door closed behind us, I knew this moment would stay etched in my memory forever. The room was filled with a soft glow as he gently laid me on the bed, his eyes never leaving mine. His touch was tender yet firm, each caress igniting a new wave of desire. Time stood still as we moved together, our bodies in complete harmony.

As I felt myself diving over the edge, I whispered. “I love you, too, Nico.”

His lips curled into a smile as he whispered back, “And I love you, my heart.” The words wrapped around us, sealing the moment with a promise. In that sacred space, we became one, as we lay entwined. I knew this was only the start of my happily ever after. We lay there, wrapped in each other’s arms, savoring the quiet intimacy of the moment. The world outside faded away, leaving only us and the unspoken promises we had made. In that moment, I felt a profound sense of peace, knowing that this was where I belonged.

26

VISITATION AND EXIT PLAN

Opening my eyes to sunlight, I rolled over to find his side of the bed empty. My body ached from the night before, yet a smile tugged at my lips, even as doubt crept in—how could love feel so real when my freedom was still stolen? I stretched gingerly, wincing as my sore muscles protested the movement. Memories of the night flooded back—his touch, the way he caressed me, and held me close. A smile tugged at my lips despite the ache. It was worth every bit of pain, and I couldn't wait to do it again. I climbed out of bed, my feet touching the plush rug, and headed into the bathroom. As I caught sight of myself in the mirror, I couldn't help but smile at the faint bruises on my skin. Each was a reminder of the passion we shared.

"Good morning, my love," he said, stepping in with a bouquet of roses. My heart fluttered at the gesture, but beneath the sweet fragrance, I couldn't ignore the weight of the unspoken chains that bound us.

I turned to him, my heart fluttering at his smile. "These are beautiful," I whispered, taking the roses.

He leans in, his lips brushing against mine. "Not as beautiful as you", he murmured, wrapping his arms around me.

I melted into his embrace, savoring the warmth of his touch. "You always know how to make me feel special," I said, my voice soft with affection.

He pulled back slightly, his eyes filled with love. "That's because you are," he replied, his tone sincere. He pulled me closer, his embrace tightening. "And I'll always make sure you feel that way." I smiled, my heart brimming with love. In that moment, I knew nothing could ever compare to the connection we shared. "Now, how does breakfast sound? Are you hungry?" He asked with a grin. "That sounds perfect," I replied, my stomach rumbling in agreement. He chuckled, his eyes twinkling with amusement. "I'll make us something delicious," he said, his voice warm and reassuring. I nodded, eager to start the day with him by my side.

"I'm just going to grab a quick shower, and I'll join you," I replied. He leaned in and kissed my forehead before leaving the room. I watched him walk away, admiring his confident stride. The sound of the shower soon filled the air, and I took a deep breath, cherishing the peaceful moment. As I prepared to join him, I couldn't help but smile, overwhelmed with gratitude for the love and happiness that enveloped our home. I took my time getting ready, savoring the anticipation of the day ahead. When I joined him in the kitchen, the aroma of freshly brewed coffee and sizzling bacon greeted me. He glanced up, his smile lighting up the room, and my heart swelled with joy. I sat down at the table as he placed a plate full of French toast and bacon in front of me.

"This looks amazing," I said, my mouth watering. He sat down across from me, his presence filling the room with warmth. We ate in comfortable silence, savoring the delicious food and each other's company. As I finished my last bite, I couldn't help but feel grateful for this perfect morning together. Just as I was about to comment on how wonderful the breakfast was, a gentle knock on the door interrupted the peaceful moment. We exchanged curious glances before he stood up to see who it might be, leaving me with a sense of anticipation.

At the door stood Drago Morelli, his presence imposing as ever. "I hope I'm not interrupting," he said with a nod, his eyes scanning the room. Nico stepped to the side, allowing him to enter, and I saw Lucianna step in right behind him. Nico's expression shifted, his brow furrowing slightly as he greeted them.

"Drago, Lucianna, what brought you here so early?" he asks, his tone polite yet cautious.

Drago's gaze lingered on me for a moment before he spoke. His voice was low and measured. "We have some business to discuss," he said. His words carried an unspoken weight. "I'm sorry, but it couldn't wait."

"Sure," Nico motioned for them to join us at the table.

"Privately," Drago responded with gritted teeth. Lucianna's presence added to the tension, her expression unreadable as she stood silently at Drago's side.

Nico hesitated, his jaw tightening before nodding and gesturing toward the study. "Let's go then," he said, his tone firm as he led them away, leaving me wondering what could be so urgent.

The study door closed behind them, leaving a heavy silence in the room. I couldn't shake the feeling that something was wrong. Lucianna's stoic demeanor and Drago's tense words hinted at trouble. Whatever they had to say, it was clear it wasn't good news. I sat there, my mind racing with possibilities. The air felt heavy with unspoken tension, and I couldn't help but wonder if this had something to do with the recent events. Whatever it was, it seemed to involve me in some way, and that thought alone made my stomach twist with unease. Just then, Lucianna and Drago re-entered the room, their expressions grave. They exchanged glances before Lucianna spoke, her voice steady but urgent. "We need to talk," she said, her eyes locking onto mine.

“There’s been an incident,” Drago added, his voice low. “I need you to come with me.”

“You are not taking her,” Nico says, drawing out his pistol and pointing it at Drago. Lucianna’s eyes widened, and Drago’s grip on my arm tightened.

“Put that away, Nico,” Drago growled, his voice steady but firm. “This isn’t the time for this.” Nico’s hand didn’t waver, his eyes locked on Drago.

“I won’t let you take her,” he insisted, his voice trembling slightly. The room was silent, the tension thick enough to cut with a knife.

“That’s enough, Nico. We weren’t just taking her away. You are coming with us, too,” Lucianna explained.

Lucianna’s words hung in the air, but Nico’s resolve didn’t falter. “I don’t trust you,” he spat, his finger tightening on the trigger. Drago’s grip on my arm loosened slightly, and I felt a surge of panic. The atmosphere was charged, and I feared any sudden move could lead to disaster.

“Listen, Nico, I don’t plan on stealing her away from you. You think it’s not obvious to me that you slept with her? Huh, I know you’ve fallen for her. But this is bigger than her, and for her safety, coming home is the right thing for both of you to do.” Drago explained.

Nico hesitated, his hand trembling as he lowered the weapon. Drago’s grip on my arm tightened again, and Lucianna stepped closer, her expression softening. “We’re not your enemies, Nico,” she said, her voice gentle but firm. “Let us help you both.”

Nico’s shoulders slumped, his grip on the weapon faltering. For a moment, the tension in the room eased, replaced by an uneasy silence. Lucianna’s words seemed to resonate, and Nico’s defiant stance wavered. “Fine,” he muttered, his voice barely audible.

Nico's gaze flicked between them, his jaw clenching as he fought to maintain control. Finally, he let the weapon drop to his side, the fight draining from him. "But if anything happens," he warned, his voice low, "it's on you. I mean it," Nico added, his voice trembling with barely contained emotion. "If anything happens to her, I won't hesitate to make you both pay." Drago nodded, his expression grave, while Lucianna's gaze remained steady, her resolve unwavering.

I followed Drago out the door, Lucianna behind. Nico was reluctant, but closed the apartment door. I spent one night inside thinking it would be my forever home. Only to realize, it wouldn't. The weight of that realization settled heavily on my chest as we walked away, leaving behind a place that had once held so much promise. "Why does she have to be taken back to the hotel?" Nico asked.

"Because it's safer there," Drago replied, his tone firm. "The hotel has security, and we can keep a closer watch. It's not ideal, but it's necessary for now." Lucianna remained silent, her expression unreadable as they continued down the dimly lit hallway. We all enter the elevator, and Drago pushes the button to the lobby.

The ride downward remained silent. Nico sighed, his frustration evident. "I just don't understand why we can't protect her here. This place feels secure enough." Drago glanced at him, his voice low but firm. "It's not about what feels secure, Nico. It's about what is secure." The elevator doors opened, and they stepped out into the lobby, the weight of their decision hanging heavily in the air.

Lucianna finally spoke, her voice soft but resolute. "It's not forever, Nico. Just until we can ensure her safety." The tension lingered as they exited the building, each step echoing the gravity of their choice.

"Listen closely, I don't want to get in between you. I am happy with my marriage. Lucianna has shown real love and understanding to me, which made me see the right way and how this was what was supposed to happen. This was the reason she became ours in the first place. To find her match, you are her match. You two make such a sweet couple." Drago said, opening the back door to a sleek black limousine.

Nico nodded, his expression softening slightly. "I know you're right, but it's hard to let go of the fear. After all, you did kidnap her and lock her in a cell with no food or water for three days. I can't just forget that happened."

Drago sighed, his gaze steady. "I know, and I'm sorry. It was a mistake, one I'll regret forever. But I promise, I'll do everything to make it right." Nico hesitated, then nodded, his resolve wavering as he stepped into the car.

27

WELCOME BACK...

As we board the private jet, I settle into one of the plush leather seats, staring out the window at the tarmac. I was heading back to where everything began, the one place where I met both men in my life. I was nervous, to say the least. I couldn't help but feel a mix of anticipation and dread. The memories of those encounters flooded my mind, each one etched with a blend of joy and pain. Returning to this place felt like stepping into a whirlwind of emotions I wasn't sure I was ready to face.

"How are you feeling, Sophia?" she asked, sitting next to me.

"I'm nervous," I admitted, my voice barely above a whisper. "It's like stepping back into a storm I barely survived the first time. But I have to go back. I know that both you and Drago have made that clear. Only I don't know what is going on. You won't tell me, and neither will Nico."

"You'll understand soon enough," she said, her tone gentle but firm. "Trust us, Sophia. This is for your own good, even if it doesn't feel like it now. Sometimes, facing the storm is the only way to find peace."

“Thanks,” I respond. I glance back out the window at the clouds floating by. The clouds seemed to mirror my inner turmoil, their shifting forms a reminder of the uncertainty ahead. As the plane descended, I gripped the armrest, bracing myself for what lay ahead. The storm was coming, and I could only hope I’d find the strength to endure it. As we exited the plane, I saw him standing there waiting, and my heart skipped a beat. Mr. Russo waited for us. He smiled at Drago and Luciana as they approached him. He smiled at Nico, and then his eyes met mine, and a chill ran down my spine. His gaze lingered on me, cold and calculating, as if he could see through my every thought. I tried to steady my breathing, but my pulse raced. Whatever awaited me, I knew it wouldn’t be easy, but I had no choice but to face it.

“Welcome home!” he said, his voice cheerful, yet his eyes betrayed a cold, calculating intent. “I’m glad to see you made it safely, and that she’s unharmed.” The words felt like a trap disguised as kindness. He escorted us to a group of cars waiting to take us back to the hotel. I avoided his gaze, focusing instead on the bustling activity around us. The tension in the air was unmistakable, and I couldn’t shake the feeling that I was walking into a carefully laid trap. My mind raced with possibilities, none of them comforting. As the car door shut behind me, I noticed I was in the back of the car alone. Where was Nico? I wondered, glancing around to find him shoved into another vehicle. The car took off, and my heart sank. I stared out the window, watching the city blur past, my mind spinning with questions. Why had Nico been separated from me? What did Mr. Russo want? The car’s silence felt suffocating, and I knew I had to stay alert. Whatever was coming, I needed to be ready.

Once we arrived at the large building, I was dragged out of the back seat forcefully. “What are you doing? Stop, you are hurting me.” I screamed at the driver as he pulled me into the building, straight to the elevator and to the basement. The driver ignored my protests, his grip tightening as he dragged me towards a dimly lit room. The door slammed shut behind us, and I heard the ominous click of a lock. My pulse quickened as I scanned the room, my eyes landing on a figure seated in the shadows.

“Well, look who it is—the one who started it all. You really are quite stunning,” he sneered, stepping into the light. I froze, my breath caught in my throat, as Zosimo Rossi emerged from the shadows.

“What?” I whispered, unsure.

“You’re the reason we’re in this mess,” he continued, his voice cold and menacing. “And now, you’re going to fix it, one way or another.” My heart raced as I tried to process his words, fear gripping me as I realized the danger I was in.

“What mess?” I asked, surprised. “What do you want me to do to fix it?” I asked in surprise, not knowing what was going on.

Zosimo’s eyes bore into mine, his expression unyielding. “You’ll know soon enough,” he said, his tone leaving no room for argument. “But understand this—your choices have consequences, and now you’re going to face them.” The weight of his words sent a chill down my spine, leaving me trembling with dread.

The door opens, and Mr. Russo steps into the room. “Listen, Sophia. We are at a complete disadvantage here as the underground demands human sale. You were the first sold, so we need you to talk to the women we captured. We need you to make them understand this is for their own good, and they have no choice. Much like you didn’t have a choice when you were sold at auction to my son-in-law,” he sighed softly.

My mind reeled as I absorbed the grim reality of the situation. “You expect me to convince them to accept this fate?” I asked, my voice trembling.

Mr. Russo’s gaze remained cold and unyielding. “It’s the only way to keep the peace,” he replied, sealing my fate.

I stared at him, my heart pounding in my chest. "And what if I refuse?" I whispered, my voice barely audible.

Mr. Russo's expression darkened. "You don't have that luxury, Sophia," he said, his tone firm and final. "Your cooperation is not optional." He motioned towards someone, and the door opened, and I saw two strong men carrying Nico. They tossed him to the floor, guns held against the back of his head. "If you refuse me, then Nico will die and you will be sold again." I felt a wave of panic wash over me as I realized the gravity of the situation. My choices were clear: cooperate and betray my principles, or resist and risk Nico's life. My heart ached with the weight of the decision I had to make. I knew what I had to do, though every fiber of my being rebelled against it. With a heavy heart, I nodded in resignation. "I'll do it," I said, my voice barely a whisper. Mr. Russo smiled coldly, his victory etched on his face.

"That's a wise girl," he said, nodding to the two men who released Nico. With my reluctant agreement secured, Mr. Russo turned to the men and issued orders in a low, commanding voice. "Prepare the women for Sophia's arrival," he instructed, his eyes never leaving mine. "And ensure that everything proceeds smoothly—any disruptions will not be tolerated." The men hurried to carry out his orders, their movements swift and precise. As they left, Mr. Russo lingered a moment longer, his gaze cold and calculating. "Remember," he said softly, "your cooperation ensures not just Nico's safety but your own survival." With that, he turned and left, leaving me to grapple with the consequences of my choice.

"I'm going to kill him for this," Nico said as he slowly stood up. Nico's voice trembled with barely contained fury. "He thinks he can control us like this? He's wrong." I glanced at him, my own anger simmering beneath the surface. Together, we shared a silent understanding—this wasn't over. The weight of Mr. Russo's words lingered in the air, a stark reminder of the power he wielded. Nico's fists clenched, his jaw tight with resolve. I knew we were both thinking the same thing—this wasn't just about survival anymore. It was about taking back control, no matter the cost.

The door opens, and several men come into the room. "Come with us," he said as he held the door open. Nico grabs my hand firmly in his, and together we follow the men back upstairs to the penthouse suite. The penthouse suite was expansive, with floor-to-ceiling windows offering a panoramic view of the city. The men ushered us inside, their expressions unreadable. Nico's grip on my hand tightened, his unease mirroring my own. The room was silent, heavy with anticipation, as we waited for whatever came next.

"I am sorry that it had to be like that." I suddenly heard Drago say as he stepped down the large stairway. The same one he carried me up several times. "You are in the same room, Nico. Go ahead and make yourself comfortable. Sophia will meet the woman tomorrow before our first human-only auction. We have twelve girls."

"What happened to you?" Nico demanded. "You lied to me!" Nico yelled, his voice trembling with anger. "You said she would be the only one."

Drago's expression remained cold, unyielding. "Circumstances change," he replied, his tone dismissive. "You know the stakes as well as I do." Nico's grip on my hand tightened, his unease palpable. I could feel the tension rising in the room, the unspoken threat hanging heavy in the air. "Now that I'm becoming the next Don, I have to come to grips with that my most critical thing is to grow my family and grow my fortune."

"You're just like the rest of them," Nico spat, his voice laced with betrayal.

Drago's eyes narrowed slightly, but he didn't flinch. "You always knew what this life demanded," he said, his voice low and steady. "You can't escape it, Nico. Not anymore, not now. I've decided you're my second-hand man. I need someone I can trust by my side," Drago continued, his gaze locked with Nico's. "You've always been loyal, but loyalty alone isn't enough. You'll learn, Nico. This is how things are now."

"I don't want this. I ran from this life. I only want Sophia. She is what matters to me," he explained.

Drago's expression hardened, his voice firm. "She's part of this now, whether you like it or not. You'll stay by my side, and together we'll protect her. But if you ever betray me, Nico, I won't hesitate to make you regret it."

Nico's jaw clenched, his eyes darting away as Drago's words settled in. "I'll never betray you," he muttered, though the bitterness in his voice lingered.

Drago nodded slowly, his gaze unwavering. "See that you don't," he said, turning away. Nico stood there, his fists clenched at his sides, as Drago walked away. He knew he had no choice but to comply, but the weight of the decision pressed heavily on him.

"Come on, Sophia. I will show you to our room," he said as he turned and headed down the hall. He opened the first door, and I entered a spacious bedroom complete with a king-sized bed, a kitchenette, and a cozy sitting area complete with a TV. I glanced around the room, noticing the elegant yet impersonal decor. I forced a small smile, trying to mask my unease. "It's nice," I said softly, though inside I felt like a prisoner in a gilded cage.

28

I KNOW EXACTLY WHAT I'M DOING (NO I DONT)

I woke the next morning to find Nico gone, and a wave of dread washed over me. As I got dressed, my stomach tightened with unease. I wasn't getting ready to meet women—I was preparing to lie to them. My goal was to convince them that this was for their benefit, even though they had no choice in the matter. I went over my speech in my head, knowing it had to be convincing. They deserved to understand the situation, even if it wasn't ideal. I needed them to trust me—or at least cooperate—for this to work smoothly.

I was dressed in a purple pantsuit and black heels, my hair pulled back into a high ponytail. Just as I finished, the door opened, and Drago walked in. His presence filled the room as he looked at me with a knowing smile. "Are you ready for this?" he asked, his voice low and steady. I nodded, trying to mask my nerves. "Let's get started then," he said, gesturing for me to follow him.

I followed him into the elevator, noting that he had pushed the button for the basement. As the elevator descended, I couldn't shake the unease building within me. The basement was dimly lit, and the air felt heavy with tension. Drago led me through a maze of corridors until we reached a steel door. He paused, glancing back at me. "This is it," he said, his tone unreadable. He unlocked the door and pushed it open, revealing a dimly lit room. Inside, a group of women sat around the room, their expressions serious. I took a deep breath, steadying myself, and stepped inside. My eyes scanned all their faces, but then I spotted one I knew. Jenny sat on the floor, her eyes hollow, and my breath caught as the room seemed to tilt around me. What was she doing here? If they knew, she was as doomed as I was.

"Jenny," I whispered, my voice barely audible.

She looked up, her eyes meeting mine with a mix of surprise and resignation. "What are you doing here?" I asked, my mind racing with questions.

She hesitated, her voice trembling slightly as she replied, "I could ask you the same thing." Her gaze shifted to the others in the room, and I could feel the tension rising. I knew I had to be careful.

"Ladies, this is Sophia Moretti. She's here to talk about what's going to happen to you. I asked her to speak with you because she understands what you're going through—she was sold at an auction just like the one happening tonight. Please listen to what she has to say; it could help keep you safe." Drago said stiffly before leaving the room, slamming the door behind him.

The room fell silent as everyone turned to look at me. I could feel their eyes on me, waiting for me to speak. I took a deep breath, steadying myself, and explained what I knew about the auction and what they could expect. I could see fear in their eyes, but I knew that I had to be honest with them. "I understand how terrifying all this feels," I said. My voice was soft but firm. "When I was in your place, I felt lost and hopeless too. I followed every direction my owner gave me, and he forced me to marry my husband. But I found love in it. He is an excellent man, and I hope you, too, can find a happy ending to this horrible fate. But I also know that not everyone's experience will be the same. What I can tell you is to stay strong, keep your head up, and never lose hope. You never know what opportunities might come your way, even in the darkest of times."

The door opened, and Drago entered, followed closely by Lucianna. Drago's expression was stern, while Lucianna's was sympathetic. They had come to escort the women to the auction, ensuring everything proceeded smoothly without interruptions. Lucianna's presence was meant to reassure them, offering a glimmer of compassion amid the chaos. I was escorted out of the room to Drago's private viewing room.

Once inside, I saw Nico, who pulled me into his arms, holding me close and safe as we both watched the auction. Nico's embrace provided a fleeting comfort, but the harsh reality of the auction loomed. As each woman was presented, their fates were sealed with every bid. The room was filled with heavy silence. Despite the grim surroundings, Nico's presence gave me hope, a small beacon in the suffocating darkness. As Jenny entered the stage, my heart raced as I watched my best friend get auctioned off in front of me. The bidding for Jenny seemed to last forever, each moment stretching my nerves to the breaking point. Finally, the hammer fell, sealing her fate. I felt a mix of relief and despair, knowing she was gone but hoping her buyer would treat her kindly. Nico's grip on me tightened, his silent strength my only anchor.

As the auction wrapped up in its entirety, Nico led me out of the private viewing room and upstairs to the penthouse suite we were now required to call home. Once inside, I felt a mix of dread and resignation. The luxury of the suite mocked the despair of our situation. Nico's silence spoke volumes, his tension mirroring my own. We were trapped, bound by circumstances far beyond our control, with no clear path to freedom. "Why don't you go and take a nap, my love. Your work is done." Nico said before meeting his lips to mine in a soft, brief kiss.

"Not too fast, there. I actually need her for something." I see De Rosa walking into the penthouse from the elevator, with Jenny fighting him as he drags her behind him.

"Let go of me!" Jenny screamed, her voice trembling with fear and anger. De Rosa sneered, his grip on her arm tightening as he shoved her towards us. Nico's eyes narrowed, his body tensed as he stepped protectively in front of me.

"What do you want from Sophia?" Nico demanded.

"I want her to talk to my girl. I purchased her to be my wife. She told me Sophia was her best friend, and she wanted to talk to her. So, that is all I want here." De Rosa smiled.

Nico's jaw clenched, his eyes burning with fury. "You're not taking her anywhere," he growled. His voice was low and dangerous.

De Rosa's smile faltered, replaced by a sneer. "Who said anything about taking her anywhere? She can talk to her here. Now."

Nico's dismissive tone put me on alert: "Sophia doesn't owe you anything, and she won't be forced into anything." De Rosa's grip on Jenny's arm loosened slightly as he assessed Nico's unwavering stance. The tension in the room thickens, the air heavy with unspoken threats.

"You're not listening," De Rosa spat, his grip on Jenny's arm tightening again. "This isn't a negotiation." Nico's eyes flickered to Jenny, then back to De Rosa. "Sophia isn't yours to control," he said, his voice steady but firm. "And you're not going to force her into anything."

"Oh, Nico, stop this and let Sophia talk to the girl. De Rosa just wants what we both have. Maybe Sophia can calm the girl down." I heard his voice and glanced at the elevator to find Drago and Lucianna stepping into the penthouse.

Nico's jaw tightened, but he didn't back down. "She talks when she's ready, not because you demand it."

The air cracked with hostility as Lucianna stepped forward. Her presence was a calming force. "Let's all breathe," she said, her tone measured. "Sophia can decide for herself."

"I will talk to her," I replied with a smile, stepping away from Nico's solid form and towards Jenny. As I approached Jenny, I could feel the tension ease slightly. Her eyes met mine, searching for reassurance. "It's okay," I said softly, placing a hand on her shoulder. "You don't have to do anything you're not comfortable with. Let's talk on the couch. You'll still be in eye view of De Rosa," I suggested.

Jenny hesitated for a moment, her eyes flickering with uncertainty, before she nodded slowly. "Okay," she whispered, her voice trembling slightly. Together, we moved to the couch, where I sat beside her, offering a reassuring smile. I could feel the weight of everyone's gaze, but I focused solely on making her feel at ease. I didn't know what to say at first, so I began with my own story, hoping it would help her feel less alone.

I told her about how I was purchased. I told her how everything was so foreign to me at first, and how I struggled to keep a strong head through it all. I shared the twists and turns of my journey and how I ultimately ended up with Nico. I told her how much I loved him, how he was everything to me, and how love had grown over time in a way I never expected.

"Being forced to marry someone is scary," I said softly, my voice filled with understanding. "You don't know if you'll ever love the man you're being tied to legally. But love does grow with time, Jenny. I have hope for you. I think you and Gio De Rosa could be great together." I smiled at her, hoping to offer her some comfort and reassurance in that moment. I hoped my words would ease her worries, even just a little. "It's not easy, but sometimes the best things in life come from unexpected places," I added, giving her hand a gentle squeeze.

"Okay, I'll stop fighting him. I have no choice here, do I?" she asked. She looked down, her voice barely above a whisper. "I guess you're right. I just wish it didn't feel so... forced." I nodded, understanding her hesitation. "It's not easy," I agreed, "but sometimes, taking a leap of faith is the first step to finding something beautiful." I glanced over at Nico, who was watching me closely. I knew she needed time to process everything, but I also believed that with patience and an open heart, she might find happiness in her new life.

29

A COUPLE OF SURPRISES!

Several days blurred into each other, each one suffocating me further. Every time I was forced to address the kidnapped women, I felt another piece of myself slip away. This was the part of my new life I despised the most. Being made to participate in something so deeply wrong. Every time I had to do it, I felt like I was losing a part of myself. I hated the way they looked at me, full of fear and desperation, as if I was one of them. It made me feel dirty, complicit in their suffering. I wanted to scream, to tell them I wasn't like the others, but I knew it wouldn't change anything.

Nico has been coerced into becoming Drago's second-in-command, a stark reminder that escaping this life might be impossible. Each day feels like a heavy chain, tightening its grip on us, suffocating any hope of freedom. In a desperate search for something—anything—to distract me from the weight of our reality, I took a pregnancy test. My body had been whispering change for days: nausea, soreness, a quiet hope I dared not name. The test revealed what I both feared and longed for: a positive result. A baby. Our baby. My heart raced as I stared at the faint line, torn between the flicker of hope it ignited and the crushing fear of what it might mean. Could this life growing inside me be the miracle that leads us out of this darkness? Or would it only anchor us more firmly to the life we so desperately want to escape?

Stepping out of the bathroom, I see Nico pulling on his boots. I know I need to share the news, but I'm not sure how he'll react. My heart races as I take a deep breath, trying to steady myself. "Nico," I say, my voice trembling. My fingers fidget with the hem of my shirt as I search his eyes, hoping for understanding. "I have something to tell you." The words catch in my throat before I finally whisper, "I'm pregnant."

His eyes widened, and for a moment, he said nothing. Then, a slow smile spread across his face. "Really?" he whispered, reaching for my hand. I nodded, tears welling up. In that moment, the weight of our reality seemed to lift, replaced by a fragile, flickering hope. But as quickly as it came, the hope began to fade. The reality of our circumstances pressed down on us once more. How could we bring a child into this chaos? Yet, even amidst the doubt, a small flame of determination flickered within me.

"What do we do?" I asked him.

He squeezed my hand, his gaze steady. "We'll figure it out," he said, his voice firm. "Together." I nodded, clinging to his words like a lifeline. Maybe, just maybe, this child could be the light we needed in our darkness. "I have to go, my love. I am late for a meeting. Drago is meeting with the board of directors that runs the hotel. He's making changes. Stay here in the penthouse. You're safe here," he urged me with a kiss on my forehead. I watched him leave, his words echoing in my mind. The weight of uncertainty lingered, but so did a flicker of hope. Together, we would face whatever came next. For our child, for us, we would find a way through the chaos.

I decided to eat something, so I headed out of Nico's and my bedroom toward the kitchen area to make myself something to eat. There, sitting at the dining table, was Lucianna. She sipped a cup of coffee. She looked up as I entered, her expression unreadable.

"Morning," she said, her voice neutral. I nodded in response, unsure of what to say. The tension between us was palpable, but I focused on making my breakfast, determined not to let it affect me. "How are you, Sophia?" she asked.

"I'm doing okay," I replied, keeping my tone even. "Just trying to settle into everything." She nodded, her gaze lingering on me for a moment before returning to her coffee. I finished making my breakfast in silence, the unspoken words hanging heavy in the air between us. I settled into one of the empty seats at the table and ate my eggs and bacon. The silence stretched on, broken only by the clinking of the cutlery on the plate. I could feel Lucianna's eyes on me, though I avoided looking up. Finally, she spoke again, her voice soft this time. "I have some news to share with you, Sophia. I hope you will help me with it."

I nodded, not trusting myself to speak. "Of course," I said, setting down my fork. "What is it?"

She hesitated, then took a deep breath. "I'm pregnant," she said, her voice barely above a whisper. "I hope you can help me through this new part of my life."

I felt a mix of emotions wash over me—surprise, confusion, and a twinge of something I couldn't quite place. "Of course, I'll help in any way I can," I managed to say, forcing a smile. She gave me a small, grateful nod. "But I feel I must share with you the news I just found out this morning as well," I say, hesitating to share my own news. "Luci, I'm pregnant too."

"What?!" she exclaimed, her eyes wide with shock. "Are you serious?" I nodded, a nervous laugh escaping my lips. For a moment, we just stared at each other, the weight of our shared news sinking in. Then, unexpectedly, we both burst into laughter, the tension breaking like a wave. We sat there, laughing until tears streamed down our faces, the sheer absurdity of the situation overwhelming us. When the laughter finally subsided, we shared a knowing look, realizing that this unexpected twist would bond us in ways we couldn't yet imagine. Together, we were embarking on a journey neither of us had planned, but one we would navigate side by side.

"What is going on here?" I heard a soft, sweet voice and glanced over to find Jenny standing in the doorway of her shared room with De Rosa.

"Oh, nothing much," Luci replied, her voice laced with humor. "Just a couple of surprises." She gestured to me with a playful smile. "Looks like we're both in for quite the adventure."

Jenny's eyes darted between us, her curiosity piqued. "Surprises, huh?" she said, raising an eyebrow. "Care to elaborate?"

Luci and I exchanged glances, our laughter still lingering. "Let's just say," I replied, "life has a funny way of keeping things interesting. Seems like we are both expecting!"

"Expecting what?" Jenny asked, her eyes widening.

"Babies!" Luci exclaimed, her smile brightening. "We're both pregnant and due weeks apart!"

Jenny's jaw dropped, and then she burst into laughter. "Well, this is definitely an adventure! Congrats to you both!" She said with a full smile as she settled into one of the empty seats herself. De Rosa walked into the room, his face full of dissatisfaction as he saw the three of us sitting at the table laughing.

"What's going on here?" De Rosa asked, his tone sharp.

Luci grins. "We're celebrating some good news. Jenny was kind enough to join us."

He frowned, clearly annoyed. "Well, I hope you're not forgetting we have work to do."

Luci's smile faltered. "Of course not," she said. Her voice suddenly became serious. "We were just taking a quick break."

De Rosa's expression softened slightly. "Alright," he said, nodding. "But let's get back to it."

I watched as Lucianna stood up, excusing herself. She left the room. "Jenny, once you've eaten, get back to our room. You must stay there while I take care of what I've been asked to do." He said, before he left the penthouse through the elevator. I watched as Jenny slumped in her chair, happiness leaving her face.

"I understand, Gio," she said, standing up and going into the kitchen to make herself something to eat. She returned shortly with a plate of food, eating quietly at the table. After finishing, she stood up and walked towards the room, her steps slow and heavy. She paused at the door, glancing back at me with a small, forced smile before disappearing inside. Leaving me alone in the large penthouse's main room. I stood up and headed into the bedroom I shared with Nico when the elevator chimed, signaling someone had arrived. I hesitated, unsure if I should wait or head to my room. The chime echoed again, breaking the silence. Curiosity got the better of me, and I moved toward the elevator, wondering who could be arriving at this hour.

When the doors opened, I immediately put myself on alert. Unsure of what to do, I didn't recognize any of the guys standing inside. They looked intimidating, dressed in dark suits, their expressions serious. I hesitated, unsure if I should speak or retreat. One of them stepped forward, his gaze scanning the room before landing on me. "Is Nico here?" he asked, his voice low and commanding.

"No, he's not here right now," I replied cautiously, my voice barely steady.

The man's eyes narrowed slightly, and I felt a chill run down my spine. "Do you know when he'll be back?" he asked, his tone leaving no room for hesitation. I shook my head slowly, trying to keep my composure.

"I'm not sure," I say, my voice trembling slightly. The man's gaze lingered on me for a moment before he nodded and stepped out of the elevator.

The man with him stepped into the penthouse. "May I ask, who are you?" he asked me with a smirk.

"I'm his wife," I said, trying to sound confident.

The man's smirk widened, and he nodded slowly, assessing me. "Alright then," he said, his voice low. "You're coming with us." The men stepped closer, and I felt a wave of unease wash over me.

I took a step back, my heart racing. "What do you want with me?" I demanded, trying to sound braver than I felt.

The man's smirk didn't waver. "Let's just say we have some unfinished business with Nico, and you're our ticket to him."

30

POSSESSION

I glanced around, searching for an escape route, but the men blocked my path. "Nico doesn't care about me," I said, my voice trembling slightly. "You're wasting your time."

The man's laugh was cold and devoid of humor. "Oh, we'll see about that." One of the men reached out and grabbed my wrist in a firm grip. I tried to pull away, but his hold only grew tighter. Panic surged through me as my heart pounded. The other men closed in, their faces hard and unyielding. I knew I had to act quickly, but my options were slipping away with each passing second. Taking a deep breath to steady myself, I summoned a burst of energy, wrenching my arm free and darting to the side, slipping through a narrow gap between two of the men. For a fleeting moment, I thought I might escape. But then a heavy hand clamped down on my shoulder, spinning me around. "You're not going anywhere but with us," the man said with a cruel grin. My hands were pulled behind my back, and I felt a rope tighten around them. I struggled against the bindings, but it was futile. The men dragged me forward, their grip unyielding. My mind raced, desperate for a way out, but the odds seemed insurmountable. Fear gripped my throat as I realized the full extent of the danger I was in.

They led me back to the elevator, pushing the lobby button. The ride was spent silently. The doors slid open, revealing a bustling lobby. My captors tightened their hold, steering me toward the exit. Desperation clawed at me as I scanned the crowd for a familiar face, anyone who might help. But there was no one. The cold air hit me as we stepped outside, sealing my fate. I was shoved into the back of a waiting car. The engine roared to life, and the car sped off. I strained against the ropes, my wrists raw from the effort, but it was no use. The city buildings blurred into the distance, fading as we left civilization behind. I was alone, trapped, and utterly helpless. The car eventually stopped in a remote, desolate area. The door opened, and rough hands pulled me out. My heart pounded as I was dragged toward a dirty, deserted building. The silence was broken only by my own breath, shallow and panicky.

"Who do we have here?" I heard a deep voice growl out. A man stepped forward, his face hidden in shadows. "Looks like we've got ourselves a guest," he sneered, his voice dripping with malice. My pulse raced as I realized the danger I was in. I struggled harder, but the ropes only dug deeper into my skin.

"We do, sir." I heard one of the men say. "Says she's his wife."

The man stepped closer, his breath hot on my face. "His wife, you say?" he muttered, his voice laced with menace. "Well, that makes things interesting." He leaned in, his grip tightening on my arm. "Let's see how much you're worth to him." The man's grip tightened further, and I could feel the panic rising in my chest. "You're going to be a nice little bargaining chip," he sneered, his voice cold and calculating. My mind raced, searching for a way out, but I was completely at their mercy.

They drag me into the building, forcing me onto a cold metal chair that sends shivers through my entire body as they bind me to it. The dimly lit room feels suffocating, the air thick with an almost palpable tension. I hear muffled voices, but my thoughts are racing too fast to make sense of them. I try to steady myself, to think clearly, but the fear is overwhelming. What does Nico owe these men? Why would they do this to me? I wonder, my mind scrambling for any possible way to escape. The room spins as I struggle to focus, my heart pounding in my ears. The men's voices grow louder, their words sharp and threatening. I feel utterly helpless, trapped in a nightmare with no escape. My only hope is Nico—but what if he can't save me?

"Marco, please send him a message." The leader laughs as they all leave me alone, tied to this metal chair. My chest tightens as I hear footsteps fading, leaving me in eerie silence. The cold metal bites into my skin, and I strain against the bindings, but they won't budge. Panic surges as I realize how vulnerable I am. I can only wait, praying Nico gets the message in time.

The next day…

I opened my eyes, scanning the dark room around me. I knew I was in trouble. What was I going to do? I was tied to a metal chair and confined to a dark room. A group of men kidnapped me, saying they wanted revenge on my husband. I try to think of a way out, but my mind is foggy with fear. The silence is deafening, and I can't stop trembling. All I can do is hope Nico gets here soon.

"I brought you something." I heard the deep voice growl and looked up to see the leader stepping into the room, holding a bowl in his hands. He pulls up another chair and sits right in front of me. "I brought you something to eat." He smiled, holding up the bowl. I watched as he pulled out the spoon. On it was a spoonful of gooey slop.

"What is that?" I asked, disgusted.

"It's oatmeal," he says, shrugging his shoulders.

I recoiled at the sight of the slop, my stomach churning with unease. "I'm not hungry," I muttered, trying to keep my voice steady.

The leader's smile widened, his eyes cold and calculated. "You'll eat," he said, his tone leaving no room for argument. "Open up," he ordered, bringing the spoon closer to my lips. I turned my head away, refusing to comply. His grip tightened on my chin, forcing me to face him. "You don't want to make me angry," he warned, his voice low and menacing.

"I don't want to make you angry," I repeated, my voice trembling. "But I can't eat that."

He stared at me for a moment, his grip still firm on my chin. Then, with a sigh, he lowered the spoon. "Fine," he said, standing up. "But you'll regret it." He turned and walked away, leaving me alone with my thoughts.

I sat there, trembling, wondering what would happen next. Would he force me to eat it later? Or would he punish me for refusing? I didn't know, but I knew one thing for sure: I couldn't trust him. As the door closed behind him, I battled with my own fear and defiance. Part of me wanted to keep resisting, to hold onto whatever shred of autonomy I had left. But another part of me worried about the consequences of my stubbornness, knowing that my situation could worsen at any moment. The tension between my will to fight and the instinct to survive weighed heavily, leaving me trapped not only by my physical constraints but also by the turmoil within.

Eventually, the leader steps back into the room, followed by his men. They all stood there, their eyes fixed on me, as if waiting for a reaction. The leader's expression was unreadable, but the tension in the room was palpable. My heart raced as I tried to steady my breathing, unsure of what they had planned. "So we have reached the end of our time. We haven't received a response from Nico about having you. And now, we must decide what to do with you.

His silence leaves us with no choice." His voice was cold, sending a chill down my spine. I knew whatever came next wouldn't be good. The leader's words hung in the air as I braced myself for what was to come. The men around him shifted slightly, their anticipation mirroring my own dread. I knew I had to choose my next move carefully, but the options felt suffocatingly limited.

"Please, don't hurt me." I pleaded with him. "I'm pregnant."

The leader's expression softened momentarily, his usual coldness giving way to a flicker of uncertainty. The room grew still, the men exchanging hesitant glances. "Pregnant?" he muttered, his voice barely audible, as if weighing the implications. The tension was palpable as he processed the information. "Well, that changes things," he said, his tone shifting to something almost remorseful. "We can't risk it. Take her to my house and keep her under watch until we know more." The men exchanged uncertain glances before reluctantly complying. As they led me away, a heavy sense of unease settled over me. My fate still felt precarious, hanging by a thread, controlled by forces far beyond my reach.

Shoved into another car, I sat in silence, the air thick with unspoken tension. I stared out the window, watching the world rush by in a blur, each passing moment feeling like an eternity. My thoughts raced with possibilities, none of them comforting. Finally, the car slowed to a stop in front of a sprawling mansion, its grandeur both awe-inspiring and intimidating. As the doors unlocked, I took a deep breath, steeling myself for whatever lay beyond those imposing walls.

The foyer was a display of opulence, with marble floors gleaming under the light of a massive crystal chandelier. Rich tapestries adorned the walls, and intricate wooden paneling added an air of timeless elegance. As I was led deeper into the mansion, the lavishness continued with plush carpets, luxurious furnishings, and rooms that seemed to stretch endlessly, each more extravagant than the last.

They pushed me into a luxurious bedroom. The door slammed shut behind me, leaving me alone in the opulent space. The silence was suffocating, broken only by the faint ticking of a clock. I scanned the room, taking in the plush bed, velvet drapes, and ornate furniture, but my thoughts were consumed by the uncertainty of my fate. My heart raced as I paced the room, searching for any means of escape. The weight of my situation pressed down on me, and I couldn't shake the feeling that I was being watched. The silence grew heavier, and I braced myself for what might come next.

31

MY KNIGHT IN SHINING ARMOR!

I nearly jumped as I opened my eyes, finding the leader standing over me. He smiled as he studied me while I slept. "What the hell are you doing?" I screamed at him. "How long have you been standing there?" I asked, my heart racing. I sat up on the bed, the blanket rumpling as I moved.

"I was just checking on you," he said calmly, his smile never wavering. "You looked so peaceful, I didn't want to wake you." His casual demeanor only heightened my unease, and I couldn't shake the feeling that something was off. "I finally got confirmation. Nico received my message about you," he laughed. "And he's on his way here now," he added, his tone light but his eyes sharp.

"Really?" I exclaimed, delighted about the news. Finally, Nico can rescue me from this nightmare.

"Not so fast, he's paying the price for what he did. But I have no intention of returning you. Not until I have his child," he laughed even louder.

"What?" I gasped. My joy turned to horror. "You can't do that!" I struggled to keep my voice steady, but panic rose in my chest. "You're insane," I whispered, my mind racing for a way out. "You'll never get away with this," I said, trying to sound confident despite the fear gripping me. His laughter echoed in the room, sending chills down my spine. I had to find a way to escape before it was too late.

"Oh, sweetheart. I already have."

I had to think fast. My only hope was to outsmart him, to find a weakness I could exploit. I took a deep breath, steadying myself, and forced a calm smile. "You may think you've won," I said, "but you have no idea what Nico is capable of. He's coming for me, and when he does, you'll regret ever crossing him." I held his gaze, hoping my bravado would mask my fear. His smile faltered for a moment, replaced by a flicker of uncertainty. "Nico doesn't forgive betrayal and always gets what he wants. You think you're in control, but you're not. He'll find us, and when he does, your fate will be sealed." I clenched my fists, praying my words would shake his confidence enough to buy me some time.

"You're wrong, young lady. He will pay for what he took from me. You and that child are his price, and he will pay it with his life." He laughed before leaving the room. I stood there, trembling, as his laughter echoed throughout the room. My mind raced, searching for a way out. I had to stay alive for Nico, for our child. I wouldn't let this man win. I had to think fast. There had to be a way to turn the tables on him. I couldn't let fear consume me. I needed to stay strong, for Nico, for our child. I took a deep breath and steadied myself, preparing for my next move. No matter what it took, I would protect my child from this madness. I couldn't let him use us as pawns in his twisted game. Every fiber of my being was focused on finding a way to break free and ensure my child's safety.

Just then, a man burst into the room, commanding immediate attention. He quickly assessed the situation, his eyes locking with mine, offering a glimmer of hope. "Oh my god, you are alive. I am so glad." I heard him say. "We've been searching everywhere for you. You're safe now," he said, his voice steady and reassuring. "We won't let him harm you or your child. Let's get you out of here."

"Who are you?" I asked, refusing to leave with just anyone. Nico would have given him something to prove he was on his side. I just knew it.

"I'm here to help," he said, holding up a small object. "Nico sent me. "He wants to make sure you're safe."

It was a silver locket, intricately engraved with a delicate pattern I recognized immediately. Inside, there was a tiny photograph of Nico and me, taken on a sunny day that seemed like a lifetime ago. This was the proof I needed, a tangible connection to the man I trusted with my life. I hesitated for a moment, then nodded. "Okay," I said, my voice trembling. "Let's go." I took a deep breath, steadying myself as I followed him out of the room. The locket felt warm in my hand, a reminder of Nico's presence even in his absence. Together, we moved swiftly, the sound of our footsteps echoing through the empty hallway.

"Not so fast, that woman belongs to me." I hear a deep voice rumble from a dark room, before we are surrounded by men in black suits. "She's not going anywhere." The locket felt heavy in my hand as I clutched it tightly, my heart pounding in my chest. The men in black suits closed in around us, their cold eyes fixed on me. "She's not going anywhere," the deep voice repeated, sending a shiver down my spine.

I glanced at the man beside me, his face determined. "We have to get out of here," he whispered urgently. "Nico is waiting for us. We'll run for it," he said, gripping my arm. "Stay close." The men moved in, their footsteps echoing menacingly. I nodded, clutching the locket tighter, as we braced ourselves to break through the circle. With a sudden burst of energy, we sprinted forward, dodging the grasping hands of our pursuers. The hallway blurred around us as adrenaline fueled our every step. The man beside me led the charge, weaving through the narrow spaces with precision while I followed, my heart racing. The men shouted behind us, but we pushed on, adrenaline driving us to the exit we desperately sought.

The sound of the gunshot scared me, and I froze as I watched the man's body drop lifelessly to the ground. I screamed, my voice echoing through the hallway as the men closed in. Panic surged through me, but I forced myself to move, clutching the locket tighter. Nico was waiting, and I had to keep running. I stumbled through the corridor, my breath coming in ragged gasps as I fought back tears. Desperation clawed at my insides, urging me to keep moving despite the chaos behind me. I ducked into an adjacent hallway, hoping to lose the men in the maze of corridors, my mind racing for a plan to escape this nightmare. I rounded a corner, my legs aching with exhaustion, and spotted a door slightly ajar. Without hesitation, I slipped inside, pressing my back against the wall, my chest heaving. The faint sound of footsteps grew distant, and for a moment, I allowed myself to hope.

"I told you there was no escaping me," I heard the leader say, before his stone-hard grip gripped my wrist, and I was pulled to the ground. I tried to scream, but his hand clamped over my mouth, muffling my cries. My heart pounded as he dragged me closer, his grip unyielding. The locket slipped from my grasp, clattering to the floor, its faint tinkle drowned by the sound of my despair. I struggled against his hold, my strength waning as panic surged through me. The room blurred as tears filled my eyes, my mind racing for any chance of escape. Then, a faint creak echoed—a door opening behind us. A voice called out, sharp and commanding, cutting through the silence.

"Let her go, Marco. Your business is with me, not my wife." I heard Nico's deep, masculine voice boom out of the room. Marco's grip loosened slightly as he turned toward the voice. Seizing the moment, I twisted free and scrambled away, my hand reaching for the locket. Nico's steely gaze locked on Marco, his presence commanding the room. "You won't touch her again," he growled, his voice low and dangerous. Marco hesitated, his eyes darting between Nico and me. Nico's voice dropped lower, colder. "You've made your choice, and now you'll answer to me." Marco's grip faltered completely as Nico advanced, his steps deliberate, his focus unwavering. Fear flashed in Marco's eyes as he backed away, realizing the gravity of his mistake.

Nico pulls out his gun and points it at Marco. "What made you think you could kidnap my wife from the safety of my home?"

Marco's face paled as he stammered, "I—I didn't think you'd find out."

Nico sneered, "You underestimated me, and that's your last mistake." The room fell silent as Nico's finger hovered over the trigger, his resolve unyielding. Marco's eyes widened as Nico pulled the trigger, the sound echoing through the room. Marco crumpled to the floor, his body still. Nico lowered the gun, his gaze cold and unapologetic. "No one threatens my family," he said, his voice steady and resolute. Nico turned on his heels; his expression was hard as stone. "Get rid of him!" He ordered. His tone left no room for argument. The others in the room scrambled to obey, their movements quick and silent. Nico's gaze lingered on Marco's lifeless form for a moment before meeting mine. "Are you okay?" He asked softly. Without waiting for my response, Nico wrapped his arms around me, pulling me into a firm embrace. I could feel the tension in his muscles, but his touch was gentle, offering a sense of security amidst the chaos. "I won't let anyone hurt you," he whispered, his breath warm against my ear. I nodded, feeling a mixture of relief and unease. Nico's grip on me loosened, and he stepped back, his eyes searching mine. "You don't have to worry about anything anymore," he said, his voice firm. "I'll handle everything." He gently took my hand and led me through the dimly lit hallway, past the ornate furnishings that seemed to cast shadows of their own. As we exited the mansion, the cool night air enveloped us, and I felt a sense of freedom begin to replace my earlier fears.

There was his sleek black car waiting. He helped me into the passenger seat before getting behind the wheel. The engine roared to life as he started the car, and we pulled away from the mansion, leaving behind the chaos and uncertainty. I glanced at Nico, his jaw set in determination, and I wondered what awaited us next.

32

HAPPILY EVER AFTER!

Back in the penthouse, "Oh man, am I glad you found her." Drago said as Nico told him what had happened at the mansion.

"Marco is dead." Nico admits to him, "No one steals what's mine and lives to see another day."

"And he won't be the last," Drago replied, his voice cold and determined. "We'll make sure of that. No one crosses us without paying the price." Nico nodded, knowing they had to send a clear message to anyone who dared to challenge them. I wasn't sure how to feel, but I knew being in his life would be filled with danger and uncertainty. I was certain that countless people were waiting for a chance to strike. I couldn't help but feel vulnerable and unsure about my safety anymore. On one hand, the thrill of being part of such a powerful and influential circle was undeniable, but on the other hand, the constant threat of violence and betrayal loomed large. I found myself questioning whether the allure of this life was worth the risk. Deep down, I wondered if I had the strength to navigate this treacherous world without losing myself in the process.

Feeling his arms wrap around my waist, I am enveloped in Nico's warm embrace before he gently places a kiss on my forehead. "You should go and rest, take care of yourself and the baby," he whispers softly in my ear. "I made an appointment with the doc to check on you both in the morning."

I nod, a mix of gratitude and unease washing over me. As much as I appreciate his concern, I can't shake the feeling that even moments of tenderness are overshadowed by the ever-present danger surrounding us. I smile at him before making my way to our bedroom. I lie on the bed and close my eyes, but my mind races with thoughts of what the future might hold. The weight of uncertainty presses down on me, making it difficult to find solace even in the quiet of the night. The bedroom is dimly lit, with soft, ambient light filtering through the curtains, casting gentle shadows on the walls. The air is filled with the faint scent of lavender, intended to soothe and calm, yet it does little to ease my restless mind. The room is a refuge of comfort and luxury, with plush pillows and a warm, inviting duvet, but even here, the tension of our world outside seeps in, leaving a lingering sense of unease. I can't help but imagine all the scenarios that could unfold, each one more daunting than the last. What if something happens to Nico, leaving me to navigate this perilous path alone? Or worse, what if our child is dragged into this world of danger and deceit? The thought of raising a child amidst such chaos terrifies me, and I wonder if it's even possible to shield them from the shadows that threaten to engulf us. Just then, Nico steps into the room, his presence a momentary balm to my spiraling thoughts. His calm demeanor and reassuring smile remind me that we're in this together, no matter what challenges lie ahead.

He slowly climbs onto the bed, wrapping his arms around my waist, pulling me against his chest. His touch grounds me, offering a fleeting sense of peace amidst the chaos. I lean into him, drawing strength from his steadiness. He meets his mouth to mine, pulling me into a heart-stopping kiss. "I thought I lost you, Sophia. I thought you were dead," he admitted in a whisper.

"But you're here now, and that's all that matters," I whispered back, my voice trembling with a mix of fear and relief. His grip tightened, as if he, too, needed the reassurance that we were both still here, still together, despite the looming uncertainty that surrounded us.

"I know I have a never-ending list of enemies, but I promise this won't happen again. Drago and I have doubled security in the hotel," he explained. "I'll do everything in my power to keep you safe," he said, his voice firm with determination. "You're my world, Sophia, and I won't let anyone take that away from me." His words wrapped around me like a protective shield, easing the tension in my chest, even if only for a moment. I wanted to believe him, to trust that his promises could keep the danger at bay. But the weight of our reality pressed down, reminding me that safety was never guaranteed. Still, his touch, his words, gave me a fragile hope to hold onto.

7 months later...

"Push, Sophia... you can do this!" I heard Nico coach me as I struggled to push our baby through my canal. The pain was overwhelming, but Nico's voice kept me focused. With one final push, I heard the cry of our baby, and relief flooded through me. Nico's tearful laughter filled the room as he whispered, "You did it. He's perfect." In that moment, everything else faded away. Tears streamed down my face as I held our newborn son, his tiny fingers curling around mine. Nico's hand found mine, his grip steady and warm. In that moment, I knew we had created something beautiful, a love stronger than any fear.

Pain starts in my stomach. The doctor rushed forward, grabbing the baby in my hands. I glanced up at Nico in fear, as the doctor looked down in fear. "We need to get her to surgery!" The doctor's urgency sent a chill through me. Nico squeezed my hand tighter, his eyes locked on mine, trying to steady us both. The room blurred as panic rose, but his voice broke through the chaos. "You're going to be okay. We're going to get through this, Sophia." I am whisked out of the room so fast. "She's hemorrhaging," I heard the doctor say as the bed moved quickly down the hallway. The pain intensified, but Nico's voice anchored me. As they rushed me into surgery, I clung to his promise. The chaos around me faded, replaced by a fierce determination to survive. For Nico, for our son, I had to fight.

Staring up into the bright light, all I could think about was the doctor placing a clear mask over my mouth and nose. He told me to count to a hundred. I could think of my family and how perfect it was now that it was complete. I closed my eyes, focusing on each breath, letting the numbers guide me into the unknown. One... two... three... The world slipped away, but my love for them burned brighter, a beacon of hope pulling me through the darkness. I drifted into unconsciousness, my heart heavy with love and fear. Each breath felt like a lifeline, connecting me to Nico and our son. The darkness enveloped me, but their faces remained vivid in my mind, fueling my will to survive. I had to make it back to them.

Opening my eyes, I could feel a warm hand holding onto mine. It was Nico's, his grip firm yet gentle. His eyes, filled with worry and love, met mine. "You're awake," he whispered, his voice trembling but steady. I squeezed his hand back, reassurance flowing between us. In that moment, I knew I had made it back to them. "Would you like to hold our son?" he asked. I nodded, my heart swelling with love and gratitude. Nico gently placed our son in my arms, and as I looked into his tiny, perfect face, I knew that every moment of pain and fear had been worth it. We were together, and that was all that mattered.

The doctor had mentioned I would need to stay in the hospital for a few days, so together, Nico and I decided on a name for our son. We chose Lucas, a name that symbolizes light and strength—perfect for the little boy who had already brought so much hope into our lives. When I was cleared to leave, Nico brought in the car seat, and we carefully bundled Lucas into it before heading home.

"I have a surprise for you," Nico said with a smile. "We're not going back to the penthouse. Drago and I purchased a mansion where we can safely raise our families together. Lucianna had a baby girl two days ago, and she's excited to meet Lucas and help you get settled into the home." His voice was warm, filled with excitement and pride.

As we drove, I couldn't help but feel a mix of emotions—the weight of the past months, the challenges we had faced, and the overwhelming love I felt for our son. Nico's hand found mine, his grip steady and reassuring. I looked at him, his eyes filled with determination and love, and I knew we were going to be okay.

When we arrived at the mansion, I was struck by its beauty—a sprawling estate surrounded by lush gardens, a place that felt like a sanctuary. Lucianna greeted us at the door, her baby girl cradled in her arms. "Welcome home," she said warmly, embracing me.

As we stepped inside, I felt a sense of peace wash over me. This was more than just a new home—it was the beginning of a new chapter for our family. A chapter filled with hope, love, and the promise of a brighter future.

ACKNOWLEDGEMENT

I want to thank:

My Husband.

My Mama.

Both my Dads.

My Grandpa.

My best friend, Lynn.

My children Kylee, Asher, Skye, and Owen.

My niece, Amelia, who strives to be a writer as well... and believe me, she will. She's an amazing young writer with good and creative ideas brewing around her head.

To all other family members who believed in me and put up with helping me with storylines and discussing the stories always playing in my head.

I want to thank EVERYONE on my Franklin team who helped make this book happen, especially my amazing manager, Michelle Estor.

www.ingramcontent.com/pod-product-compliance
Lightning Source LLC
LaVergne TN
LVHW090608110826
845146LV00001B/304

* 9 7 9 8 8 9 3 2 4 8 8 6 9 *